PM

Alys tried to li

'Well, you do have a reputation for leading girls astray. . .'

Zack was rapidly losing patience with the gossips, and was annoyed with his failure to resist her tug at his emotions. Falling in love with little miss innocence was no part of his plans for the future!

'I suggest you take what gossiping juniors say about me with a large pinch of salt and rely on your own judgement, Nurse Mackenzie,' he said coolly.

We hope you'll love the forthcoming new look for medical romances. From next month—bright new covers, bright new name, and, of course, the same great stories with a medical theme, for you to enjoy—all from Love on Call.

THE EDITOR

Dear Reader

This month we offer you Accident and Emergency, Cardiac, Physiotherapy, and a holiday resort in Egypt — how's that for variety? Lynne Collins gives us a hero who is dogged by gossip, Lilian Darcy an older heroine coping with passion for a younger man, Drusilla Douglas a heroine confused by identical twins, and Margaret Barker gives us a pair who had met before. . .

    We hope you enjoy learning how they solve their problems!

The Editor

Lynne Collins' many Medical Romances are based on personal experience of hospital life, backed by research and information from her many friends in the medical profession. She likes writing about hospital settings for their wealth of human interest. Married with one son, she now lives on the Essex coast, and enjoys travel, meeting people, talking, walking and gardening.

Recent titles by the same author:

OUT OF PRACTICE
HEART IN CRISIS
REPENTANT ANGEL

HEART ON HOLD

BY

LYNNE COLLINS

MILLS & BOON LIMITED
ETON HOUSE   18–24 PARADISE ROAD
RICHMOND   SURREY   TW9 1SR

*First published in Great Britain 1993
by Mills & Boon Limited*

© Lynne Collins 1993

*Australian copyright 1993
Philippine copyright 1993
This edition 1993*

ISBN 0 263 78342 1

*Set in 10 on 12 pt Linotron Times
03-9309-50241*

*Typeset in Great Britain by Centracet, Cambridge
Made and printed in Great Britain*

CHAPTER ONE

A SUMMER storm erupted as she got off the bus and Alys ran through a bright flash of lightning and sudden, torrential rain towards the tower block that housed Accident and Emergency as well as a number of other departments and some wards, drawing her navy cardigan about her shoulders, thick blonde hair beginning to straggle.

Damp and dishevelled, she tumbled through the swing doors of A and E and collided with the senior casualty officer, who put a steadying hand on her arm, his sweeping glance taking in the wisping curls, her rain-streaked, very pretty face and the breathlessness that betrayed her dislike of being late.

'Fire or haemmorhage, Nurse?' he drawled. 'Ah, no — merely flood, I see. You look as if you've been left out in the rain all night.'

'A greeting guaranteed to make a girl feel good!' she sparked, glowering at the amused mockery of eyes and deep voice, unaware that the rush of colour to her face left her looking prettier than ever.

Brushing past him, she sped to the changing-room to remove her damp cardigan and hang it in her locker, wishing it had been anyone but Zachary Howes who had encountered her when she was looking so bedraggled.

Many of her fellow nurses thought him fascinating,

with his lean, bronzed face, deep-set eyes and devastating smile. But Alys had seen those grey eyes harden to steel and felt the sting of his scornful disapproval on occasion, and as a result she was wary of the charm that he exercised to such good effect on everyone else.

Tucking away the straying strands of hair from her ears and over her uniform collar, she rammed a pristine white cap over thick blonde curls and secured it with a couple of pins. Then, buckling her belt about her trim waist, she hurried to report to the casualty sister.

'You're late, Nurse Mackenzie!' Wanda Nelson said coldly.

'I'm sorry, Sister. I overslept and then missed my usual bus.' Alys did her best to sound convincingly contrite.

'Don't waste my time with feeble excuses, Staff. Just get on with your work without any more delay—and try not to make a habit of missing buses!'

It was a mild rebuke for once, for the senior nurse seldom missed an opportunity to berate her. Alys bore with Wanda's obvious dislike of her with only the occasional protest or grumble for she enjoyed her present job in Casualty with all its interest and excitement even if one or two people did make life difficult for her at times.

Wanda Nelson, for one. . .and the handsome, sardonic SCO for another!

It had been fairly quiet in the department until the rain suddenly swept through the town, taking pedestrians and motorists by surprise and causing a number of mostly minor accidents.

One three-year-old patient had rushed indoors when the storm broke and fallen over a scurrying cat, hitting her head against a table. Alys mopped up the tears along with the blood and was telling little Nula a story to distract her when Zack put his dark head round the concealing curtain of the cubicle.

He smiled at the toddler. 'This is Nula, is it? What's the problem, Nurse?'

'It's just a little cut, Doctor,' she said brightly for the sake of the listening infant, who was regarding the white-coated stranger with wide, doubtful eyes. 'No sign of concussion and she hasn't been sick at all.'

Zack's long fingers gently brushed back the dark curls to explore the tender brow with its imminent bruising. Nula whimpered. 'It's all right, sweetheart. I'll do my best not to hurt and if you're a brave girl I expect I can find something nice in my pocket for you,' he promised.

'Sweeties?' Nula demanded eagerly.

Alys saw the warmly tender smile that curved Zack's sensual mouth as he nodded, and unexpectedly warmed to a man she might have judged too hastily because of grapevine gossip. Summoning a first-year to hand syringe and sutures and antiseptic wipes, she left him to his skilful stitching while she went to reassure the waiting mother.

Casualty was busy but the COs and nurses were coping well with the sudden rush of work. It was the occasions when disaster struck the general public or the local football team entertained a famous side and the supporters clashed that A and E felt overwhelmed and understaffed.

'What happened to you this morning?'

Alys turned with a smile for the fair-faced casualty officer who had challenged her with the light words. 'Overslept,' she admitted ruefully.

'Wanda's on the warpath this morning,' he warned with his pleasant smile. 'She was breathing fire when you didn't turn up first thing. I'm afraid you aren't her favourite person, Alys.' He hesitated. 'It didn't help matters when Zack pointed out that you're usually on time and a very good nurse.'

She lifted a surprised face. '*He* said that! I don't believe it!' Praise from Zachary Howes, in or out of her hearing, was a rare thing.

'You're a dark horse, Alys,' he teased. 'I suspect that you and Zack have something going that no one knows about.' The light words concealed an ongoing jealousy of a colleague who had won the plum jobs in the past that Martin had wanted for himself.

She laughed. 'If I had something going with Zachary Howes the whole of Benny's would know it! You're forgetting the grapevine — and the fact that some nurses would willingly work a whole week of extra shifts just for a date with him!'

Martin nodded wryly. 'I wish I knew what it is about Zack that makes all you girls sigh over him.'

'Not me,' Alys said firmly. 'He isn't my type.' It wasn't strictly true, she admitted, recalling that slight stir of interest. But there was no future in sighing over the handsome SCO. Having worked at a London hospital for some years, he had returned to St Benet's as SCO just as Alys transferred to A and E, and he had dated Wanda Nelson ever since, apparently having known her in earlier days. Now, the junior nurses were saying that marriage was in the air.

He was almost too good-looking with his tousle of thick black curls and lean, intelligent face and slow, warming smile. His piercing grey eyes were so perceptive that Alys sometimes felt that he could see right into the heart of her — and scorned what he saw.

'Cubicle Four, please, Staff. Patient with a head injury. I don't know how you nurses find the time to stand about gossiping!'

The sharp voice with its unmistakable underlay of dislike rang out from the other side of the bustling room, drowning the wail of a child, the swearing of a man with blood streaming from a cut above his eye and the rumble of a trolley.

Alys said hastily, 'Talk to you later, Martin. . .' and fled, receiving a sympathetic smile in passing from Nicola Hastings, another of the overworked casualty officers. It seemed to be one of those days when Wanda set out to make herself generally unpopular!

The head injury wasn't a serious one. X-rays were ordered by the examining CO and Alys set a junior to the task of cleaning blood and grime from the patient's face where she had collided with the ground after a fall from a flight of stone steps. On her way from the cubicle, she peeked into the adjoining one, where a harassed junior nurse was struggling with a screaming, kicking toddler.

Zack greeted Alys with obvious relief. 'Are you free, Staff? This young lady won't let me touch her unless you hold her.' Nula had resisted all his attempts with shrill cries of protest and a demand for 'the other nurse', and he was slightly impatient with the inability of the first-year to cope with the wilful patient. 'She seems to have taken a liking to you,' he added, the light words implying understanding of a preference for the pretty staff nurse with the lovely eyes and sweet smile.

Alys nodded a dismissal to the junior, who was only too pleased to hand over her charge. 'I expect Sister can use you somewhere else, Nurse,' she said as Nula stretched out plump brown arms to her and she lifted her from the couch. She smiled at Zack. 'Perhaps she'll be happier sitting on my lap while you suture,' she suggested, hugging the little girl to her and stroking the silky hair from her brow. 'No need to cut off any of these beautiful curls, anyway. . .' she added soothingly.

The child quietened with warmly comforting arms about her and a face she considered familiar and friendly close to her own and Zack dealt with the deep cut just below the hairline with deft, skilled fingers, standing so close that Alys was disturbingly aware of his powerful body and potent masculinity.

Sensuality seemed to emanate from him in spite of the clinical white coat and surgical gloves and the intensity of his concentration and she found it surprisingly difficult to keep her mind on the business of distracting Nula while he sutured. There was something very attractive about the tall, powerfully built man with the quiet reserve that was redeemed by the breathtaking warmth of a smile that set all the juniors dreaming. Alys had her own dreams firmly under control, fortunately.

Straightening, satisfied with the neat embroidery of his stitching, Zack was struck by the glowing tenderness in the staff nurse's eyes as she murmured comfort to the child in her arms. Contrary to rumour, he took little notice of the nurses who surrounded him during his long days in Casualty, but for some weeks now he had been noticing and admiring the looks and the warm personality of Staff Nurse Mackenzie with her fair curls and pretty, heart-shaped face.

A false accusation of sexual harassment by an unbalanced colleague at Hartlake had encouraged him to apply for the post of SCO at his home-town hospital and he had returned to Benny's with the resolve to avoid romantic involvement with any woman. But his resolution seemed to crumble slightly before the picture Alys made as she cuddled the little girl and he smiled down at her with an admiring warmth in his speaking grey eyes.

Glancing up, Alys was startled by the unexpected lurch of her heart. She reminded herself sternly that the undeniable melt of his smile had captivated many more experienced girls than herself if all the talk about Zachary Howes was to be believed. It wasn't so surprising that she should feel threatened by its tingling effect at a moment when she was temporarily off her guard, for he had a charisma and a charm that many of her fellow nurses admired.

'I think Nula has been so good that she deserves more than one sweetie, don't you, Nurse?' he said lightly and brought a handful from the deep pocket of his coat.

As the little girl picked them over and took the ones

she fancied at his invitation, Alys said with her unconsciously pretty smile, 'You seem prepared for any
eventuality. You must have been a Boy Scout at some
time!' The words made light of the moment but she
warmed to that glimpse of the thoughtful and caring
nature that made him such a good doctor.

'A sweet can work wonders for a frightened child,'
he reminded her, watching as she covered his expert
needlework with a dry dressing, admiring the pretty
profile and the soft curves of her slim figure. 'She
should be fine now,' he declared in a briskly professional tone, dragging his thoughts back to the
mundane. 'Tell the mother to bring her back next
week to have the stitches out.'

Alys bridled at the cool tone that damped her
friendly overture. 'You needn't spell it out for me, Dr
Howes. This isn't my first day in Casualty,' she told
him tartly.

Zack lifted a dark, slimline eyebrow. 'It gets to be
automatic, working with the juniors. Don't be so
touchy, Alys. I know just how long you've been
around, brightening up the place,' he assured her
warmly, regretting the unintentional offence.

Unsure whether to trust the glimmering smile in the
depths of those steel-grey eyes, Alys whisked Nula
from the cubicle and back to a relieved mother who
nodded and smiled in reply to careful instructions as if
she understood. Doubting that the Asian woman's
English was up to it, Alys wrote it down for her and
then waved goodbye to the toddler with her silky black
curls and beautiful brown eyes in a chubby face.

Her next patient was a building-site worker who had

fallen from scaffolding and broken a shoulder as well as both legs as he hit the ground. Waiting for the results of X-rays as well as the arrival of the orthopaedic consultant, the man was in obvious discomfort but seemed cheerfully resigned to a long stay in hospital.

He visibly brightened at sight of Alys and she blushed at some of his outspoken comments although four years of nursing should have inured her to the kind of male patient who thought nurses were fair game.

As the receiving CO, Martin returned to check on the patient's condition and drew back the curtains in time to hear a particularly ribald remark that made her face flame with embarrassment. Alys saw the swift spark of anger and knew that in any other circumstances the man would have felt the lash of the casualty officer's acerbic tongue.

Martin had a short fuse and was often rather protective towards her—the other nurses teased her about his obvious admiration. She liked him but she had put her heart on hold when she decided to train as a Benny's nurse and she had no intention of allowing her decision to be changed by a good-looking doctor, however nice he might be. Or how attractive, she added, crushing the kindling thought of Zachary Howes.

'Got a problem, Staff?' Martin's glance was enquiring, slightly concerned.

'Nothing I can't handle, Doctor,' she assured him, smiling.

He nodded and turned to the patient. 'How are you

feeling, Ted? Not too uncomfortable?' It was casualty
policy to use first names to put patients at their ease
and the man managed to grin as Martin put cool
fingers on his wrist. 'I've just had another word with
the orthopaedic registrar and he'll be coming to see
you very soon.'

'Can I have something for the pain while I'm waiting, Doc? It's pretty bad.' He was such a rough, tough
individual that Alys was sure he hated having to admit
to pain or ask for drugs to alleviate it, and she gave his
work-roughened hand a comforting squeeze. With a
sudden grin, he added cheekily, 'It's OK, Doc. You
needn't bother with the needle. Just leave this little
nurse here with me and close the curtains on your way
out and I'll be fine.' He winked at her meaningfully. 'I
bet you can help a man forget that he's broken a
couple of bones, eh, Nurse? And how to sweeten the
night hours for these hard-working medics?'

'I'm afraid Staff is needed elsewhere,' Martin said
smoothly. 'But I'll send along another nurse to hold
your hand.'

'She'd better be as nice as this one or I'll lodge a
complaint!' The man looked disappointed as Alys
disengaged her hand.

'All Benny's nurses are nice. It's written into their
contract of employment,' Martin returned lightly,
holding the colourful curtains aside for Alys to precede
him from the cubicle. As soon as they were out of
earshot, he smiled down at her. 'I think we should
send Nurse Webb to sit with him, don't you?' he
suggested with a gleam of mischief in his blue eyes.
'She'll soon dampen his ardour.'

Alys laughed and nodded. 'The perfect choice,' she agreed and sped in search of the plump, middle-aged nurse who had returned to nursing when the last of her children had flown the nest.

Elinor Webb's Yorkshire bluntness would soon silence the young labourer whose colourful language had dismayed Alys even though she was used to encountering all kinds of patients in Casualty.

Perhaps she was more sensitive than usual to remarks that had been meant to flatter but might have been better phrased, she thought wryly. Thankfully, it had been Martin who saw her blushes rather than the SCO. She suspected that Zack would have been amused and slightly scornful of her tender feelings. After all, she had been a nurse for long enough to develop a second skin, she reminded herself—sure that it was exactly what *he* would say with that sardonic twinkle in the grey eyes.

She glanced through the slightly open door of the office to see the SCO and the casualty sister in a tense exchange of low words. His broad back bristled with ummistakable annoyance and Wanda's head was thrown back with a hint of defiance.

Her obstinate streak was well-known and Zack's dislike of being challenged was already a byword in the department. Alys felt it might do him the world of good not to get his own way for once, whatever the couple were arguing about. It looked like a lovers' quarrel so it seemed that the path of true love wasn't running too smoothly!

She looked over her shoulder at the sharp slam of the door. As their glances collided, Zack quickened his step to catch up with the slender girl in her blue dress and crisp cap.

'Did you hear any of that?' he asked with a rueful smile, knowing it had been a waste of time to argue with someone as wilful as Wanda. She had been saying no on principle since she was a very small girl!

'I wasn't listening,' Alys returned coolly.

'You're unusually incurious for a woman, aren't you?' Zack mocked gently. 'In my experience, most nurses are all ears whenever Sister Nelson and I have a slight difference of opinion.'

Alys smiled up at him sweetly. 'I think everyone's lost interest in your relationship with Sister Nelson, Dr Howes. Most nurses are romantics who love a happy ending but it seems an unlikely event in your case.'

He laughed. 'That sounds as if you want to marry me off to Wanda. I'm afraid you're due for a disappointment, Staff. She won't have me!'

Zack forbore to mention that it was all of twenty years since he had proposed. He had been twelve at the time and the ten-year-old Wanda had turned him down with a scornful smile, but that wasn't why he was still single all these years later. He simply hadn't met a woman who mattered more than medicine — until now, perhaps.

The slender Alys Mackenzie with her pretty heart-shaped face and wary eyes seemed to be stirring an unfamiliar and not entirely welcome emotion in his breast. . .

CHAPTER TWO

ALYS missed the twinkle in the grey eyes. 'I'm not at all surprised,' she retorted drily, wondering why she felt a strange mix of dismay that he cared enough to have asked and relief that Wanda hadn't accepted. Her sidelong glance unconsciously queried his apparent lack of concern or disappointment.

'I wonder what it is that you have against me?' Zack mused, picking up the gauntlet of her obvious distrust. She probably misinterpreted his relationship with Wanda, along with everyone else, but she was so discouragingly distant that he doubted she took much interest, unlike the romantic juniors who spread so many absurd rumours about his love life.

Alys shrugged. 'It isn't a built-in rule that a nurse must like every doctor she meets in the course of her work,' she said indifferently.

'And it isn't vitally necessary to my peace of mind that every nurse I meet in the course of a day's work should like me,' he countered. 'But if I've inadvertently upset or offended someone I like to put things right. How about a heart-to-heart over a drink this evening and we'll straighten it out?'

'There's nothing to straighten out,' Alys assured him with off-putting firmness.

His sudden smile was magic. 'Then we can just enjoy a drink together. Seven o'clock at Tommo's?'

17

Vanishing into a cubicle, he drew the curtains on himself and the patient before she could agree or assert that she had no intention of meeting him that night or any other.

Alys walked on, astonished by the unexpected invitation from the attractive SCO. Somewhere deep down, so deep that she wasn't admitting it even to herself, she was gratified, too. But she suspected that it had been prompted by his disagreement with the casualty sister rather than a genuine interest, and it would be foolish to add fuel to the fire of Wanda's dislike of her by dating a man that the other girl seemed to regard as her personal property. Even if she didn't want to marry him.

Having dispatched Nurse Webb on her mission of mercy, almost sorry not to be present to see the bricklayer's face fall on her arrival, she answered an urgent call from a junior nurse to deal with a patient in the throes of an asthma attack, and Zachary Howes and his invitation were both forgotten as she hurried to set up an oxygen stand and hand the mask to the gasping woman with soothing reassurances.

But she was reminded later when she overheard Nicola and the reception clerks discussing the latest rift in the SCO's rumoured romance with Sister Cas. They sounded so sure it was only a temporary hiccup that Alys was even more convinced Zack had only paid her that trifling attention in a moment of pique.

Martin agreed with her when she impulsively confided in him over a coffee in the cafeteria. 'Steer clear of Howes,' he warned, sounding like a concerned big brother. 'I've known him for years and he eats little girls like you for breakfast!' The veiled dislike of Zack stemmed from their medical student days when he had consistently been outclassed by the man. 'Surely you know that he has a reputation?'

Alys did, of course. But gossip about a good-looking doctor was often greatly exaggerated and she doubted that the SCO's love life could be as busy as romantic junior nurses liked to imply. 'I'm not sure he's as black as he's painted, Martin,' she demurred. 'He doesn't seem to be interested in anyone but Sister Cas!'

'Well, he's broken a few hearts in his time,' he warned her brusquely. 'And I gather he left Hartlake in a hurry because of some trouble with a woman. I can't say I'm surprised.'

It was common knowledge that Martin didn't like his new boss but the harshly antagonistic tone still startled Alys. 'You needn't worry about me, Martin. I can take care of my heart,' she assured him firmly, amused by the suggestion that it could be endangered so easily.

'Famous last words,' he said drily.

She shook her head at him. 'I can't see the harm in having just one drink. . .'

'Then you're having second thoughts?'

'I didn't say that I'd meet him.'

'And you didn't say that you wouldn't,' he said perceptively. 'Well, I can only advise you against it but what you do is up to you, Alys.' He was disappointed as well as disapproving. 'I don't know what you girls see in him. Something to do with playing with fire, I suppose.'

There was some truth in the words, Alys admitted.

Zack might only be using her to punish Wanda Nelson for some unknown offence but that didn't stop her from feeling a flutter of excitement at the thought of spending some time with him away from the clinical atmosphere of A and E.

Playing with fire, indeed. . .

Having decided to resist temptation, it was a mystery to Alys why she crossed the road to Tommo's that evening instead of taking her usual bus home.

With her heart beating foolishly fast, she pushed open the door, half expecting that Zack had given up on her for she was twenty minutes late, thanks to a last-minute emergency that a probably suspicious and possibly jealous Sister had assigned to her.

Tommo's was a popular meeting place for medical students and junior nurses as well as a sanctuary for overworked senior staff, and the place was full of familiar faces. Zack was talking to Tom Jenkins, one-time head porter at Benny's, who had invested his life savings in the wine bar on his retirement. Seeing her reflection in the bar mirror, he swung on the bar stool to smile at Alys.

With every quivering fibre of her being warning her of danger, she wondered why she didn't turn tail and run for an approaching bus.

'Sorry I'm late — I wasn't sure that you'd still be here. . .' She was cross with herself for sounding like a breathless teenager and cross with Zack for making her feel like one as he led her to a corner table, the warm clasp of his strong fingers on her arm sending a shiver of awareness down her spine, the powerful height of him quickening her heartbeat.

'I just hoped you'd turn up eventually. I'm delighted that you have,' he told her with a smile that quickened her too responsive pulses.

He went up to the bar and Alys studied his dark head and the set of his broad shoulders as he waited for the drinks. The gleam of jet hair tumbling over his handsome brow and the crisp curls that nestled on the nape of his neck, inviting the tease of a woman's touch, the lean line of bronzed cheek and the sweep of strong jaw, filled her with sudden, startling longing.

It was purely physical attraction but she didn't underestimate its impact — or its dangers. Zack's dark good looks and warm smile stirred her senses against her will, defying her sensible decision to keep him at arm's length. Alys reminded herself of the rumoured women in his past and the very attractive woman in his present and knew exactly where she stood.

'I'm not sure what I'm doing here,' she said doubtfully as he set her white wine and his own innocuous beer on the table and slid beside her on the cushioned seat, his muscular thigh brushing against her own, tumbling her senses. 'After the day I've had, I should have gone home and put my feet up!'

Zack's smile was disarming. 'We've both had a long day, Alys. We're entitled to some relaxation. Why shouldn't we relax with each other?'

She looked at him with suspicion in her wide hazel eyes. 'I'm not sure that we share the same views on relaxation,' she said drily.

'A drink in pleasant surroundings, listening to music, talking. . .that's my idea of relaxation. How about you?'

It sounded just the kind of evening she most enjoyed but Alys wouldn't gratify him by saying so. 'It depends on the company,' she compromised.

'An important consideration,' he agreed lightly. 'All *I* ask for is someone who'll laugh at my jokes and show that she likes being with me and won't be too obviously bored when I talk shop.'

'Sounds just like Wanda,' she said, a little maliciously, for they seemed a mismatched couple in many eyes.

Zack smiled, knowing that he and Wanda were said to be chalk and cheese. 'Do you think so? She doesn't share my sense of humour and she hates talking shop, I'm afraid.'

'If you have so little in common, why do you want to marry her?' Alys asked impulsively and then hot colour swamped her cheeks. Friends and family were always telling her to think before she spoke! She laughed to conceal her embarrassment. 'Silly question! She's beautiful and she's sexy and you love her!'

'You could be right,' Zack returned lightly, rather amused by the rumours about himself and Wanda. She *was* beautiful and she *was* sexy but they had been friends much too long to be lovers.

He wasn't ready to admit that to the girl who sat beside him with her slim hands wrapped around each other, a guarded expression in her lovely, long-lashed hazel eyes and a defensive stillness in her slim form, for he was wary of committing himself after that experience of a woman who had made life so unpleasant for him at Hartlake that he had seized the first opportunity to get away. He had been innocent of the charge but not everyone had believed him, he knew.

Alys was surprised by the sink of her heart at the non-committal words and tone that seemed to protect his privacy. Had she really hoped, deep down, that his sudden desire for her company had its roots in a genuine liking that might lead to something more?

She reached for her wine. 'I need this after today,' she said with feeling. 'It wasn't just that we were busy. I couldn't seem to do anything right for Sister Cas!'

'I've noticed that you don't get on,' Zack agreed cautiously.

Wanda had cause to be jealous of her, he knew, for she was still deeply in love with Martin Kemp and badly hurt that he had taken fright and flight when she betrayed her wish to marry him. She refused to give up a job where she couldn't avoid seeing the young CO almost every day so, to protect her pride, Zack tolerated the rumours that had linked their names since his return to St Benet's.

She needed the caring support of a long-time friend now that Kemp was parading a hurtful interest in the pretty staff nurse and Zack hadn't bargained for his own deepening interest in the girl who obviously believed that he and Wanda were lovers. . .

'I've never known her very well,' Alys admitted. 'She's a few years older so we weren't in the same set and this is the first time that we've actually worked together.'

'Benny's is a big place,' Zack agreed. He smiled at her. 'You seem to be enjoying A and E in spite of Wanda — if *enjoy* is the right word.'

'I love it,' she told him warmly, crushing the instant reaction to the charm of his smile, seizing on a safe subject of conversation. 'I liked ward work but this is much more eventful. I like the feeling that we can put most things right for most people in a very short time, easing minds as well as pain. But it can be rather alarming that patients have so much faith in our ability to cure all their problems.'

'That's just your natural modesty,' he told her with a twinkle. 'I'm instantly outraged if anyone dares to question my ability—and some of them *do*, of course. But I expect you put that down to my well-known arrogance.'

He was teasing her but Alys was dismayed that he knew what she sometimes said about him and her face glowed with embarrassment.

Zack stifled the urge to put an arm about her and hug her reassuringly. Every instinct warned him against rushing his fences but he was strongly attracted by her piquant prettiness and sweet nature.

Alys finished her wine in a gulp and put down the empty glass. 'I must be on my way. . .'

'Surely not!' Zack protested immediately. 'I thought we'd have one more drink and then go somewhere for a meal—Indian or Chinese or whatever you prefer.'

'Sounds tempting, but I've already made other arrangements,' she fibbed firmly, determined not to encourage what could only be a casual interest. She wasn't his kind of woman and she mustn't make the mistake of thinking that she could be, she warned herself sensibly.

Zack stifled his disappointment. He was desperately

tempted by the lovely face and very kissable mouth, the curve of small breasts and slim, rounded hips and the slender, shapely legs. He wanted very much to press his lips to the scented silk of her ash-blonde curls and trail a path to a mouth that he was sure would be soft and warm and welcoming. He wanted to hold her close, stirring her to eager response, aware that a fierce desire was scorching his blood as she sat by his side.

But he hesitated to show his feelings too plainly. For the first time in his life, he was unsure, anxious not to make any false moves that might put Alys off him forever.

In his younger and less responsible days at St Benet's, his good looks had won him plenty of girls, but his attitudes had altered with maturity. In recent years, he had dedicated most of his time and energies to medicine with a view to a consultancy in due course so it had been galling to be unfairly accused of an overt sexuality in his dealings with a colleague. That kind of mud could stick.

There had been the occasional affair through the years but no serious commitment on either side and no one had been hurt. So it was irritating that the reputation he had acquired in his medical-student days still clung to him, obviously giving rise to rumours and affecting Alys's opinion of him.

He knew he had given her small cause to like him during the weeks they had worked together in A and E for he couldn't always resist a gentle mockery of the staff nurse who took herself and her work so seriously — and at other times he had come down hard on her in sheer self-defence against her insistent appeal, he admitted wryly. . .

As soon as she stepped on to her bus, having refused his offer to drive her home, Alys regretted rushing away from him with so little reason. It was all due to panic, she knew. Unused to the feelings that swamped her as she sat at his side, she'd decided that flight was the best policy.

For years, she had kept men at a distance, guarding her heart even more carefully than her virginity, wanting to be very sure before she surrendered either. She was alarmed that Zack's smile seemed to have the power to melt a little of the ice that she had packed about her heart to protect it.

Sinking into her seat, she craned for a last glimpse of him. Hands plunged deep into trouser pockets, wide of shoulder and lean of hip, he headed for the hospital car park as the bus took Alys further and further from temptation. But she carried a vivid mental image of him all the way to the modern apartment block and the flat that she shared with two friends from her early training days.

Sally was curled up on the sofa with a book that she put down as soon as Alys walked into the sitting-room. 'How did it go? Aren't you *early*? What went wrong?' she asked eagerly.

Wynne left the preparations for the evening meal to stand at the kitchen door, studying her friend with shrewd eyes. 'Don't pressure her, Sally. It was obviously a disaster,' she said perceptively.

'I don't know what you're talking about!' Alys said cagily.

'No secrets!' Sally exclaimed. 'We know just where you've been — and who with!'

'Zachary Howes. Tommo's,' Wynne confirmed.

Alys groaned. 'Who saw us?'

'Half the staff, I expect,' Sally teased. 'It isn't the most sensible place to meet if you want to keep things to yourself!'

'Martin rang and when we told him you weren't home yet he said that you'd probably gone for a drink with Zack,' Wynne admitted.

Alys was annoyed that Martin had obviously phoned to check if she'd met the SCO that evening in spite of his well-meant warnings. Dumping her shoulder-bag on a chair, she kicked off her sensible brogues and sank to the sofa. 'It was just a drink,' she said defensively. 'No need to make a big romance of it!'

'If we're talking Zack Howes, then it isn't likely to be a big romance,' Wynne said cynically, her words based on past recollections of an amorous medical student rather than present-day experience of the more mature SCO. 'More like a one-night stand!'

'I must say I admire your strong-minded attitude, Alys,' Sally teased. 'I'd have been tempted to make the most of a night out with Zachary Howes if I'd been in your shoes! He's quite the best-looking man at Benny's — and no ties!'

'Wanda Nelson,' Wynne suggested succinctly.

Sally looked scornful. 'If that was serious the whole world would know! She'd be crowing like mad and flaunting a huge ring on her finger! *I* don't think he's in love with her, no matter what people say!'

Alys suddenly felt that she had to put the record

straight. 'Well, he is,' she said flatly. 'He told me so himself.'

'One wonders how the subject arose,' Wynne said slyly, twinkling. 'Surely you didn't ask him?'

'I can't recall what we were talking about at the time,' Alys returned with evasive airiness. 'But he certainly said that he wants to marry her — and it isn't surprising, is it? She's got it all. Looks, brains, personality. . .'

'And her mother's on the hospital trust committee and he wants a consultancy,' Sally finished drily. 'That says it all!'

It was grapevine gossip and Alys had been inclined to believe it in the past, along with her friends. But now, for some inexplicable reason, she didn't want to ascribe such material motives to Zack's interest in the casualty sister. She preferred to think better of him although it meant accepting that his affair with Wanda was all down to love.

Which made her wonder all the more why he had wanted to take *her* out that evening. . .

She reported for duty the following morning just as an ambulance trolley hurtled through the outer swing doors of A and E, heading for the emergency-room. As the crash team swung into action, the patient's weeping wife was led away by a junior nurse with the promise of a nice cup of tea.

The casualty sister beckoned to Alys. 'Give a hand here, please, Staff!'

Still adjusting her cap on her unruly curls, she followed to find a junior doctor working on the patient while Nicola inserted a cannula into a vein. Alys

checked pulse and blood-pressure readings while
Wanda sorted out monitor leads and another CO
plugged in the defibrillator.

'All right, Chris—stop! Asystole!' Nicola suddenly
exclaimed. 'Calcium and adrenalin!'

Alys handed her a prepared syringe and the CO
located the right place on the man's flaccid chest before
plunging the needle directly into the failed heart.
Waiting for a sign that the life-saving drugs cocktail
had done its job, Chris Mortimer continued with his
steady, rhythmic pumping.

'Nothing,' Wanda reported, already reaching for the
paddles of the defibrillator. Everyone stood back as
the powerful charge shot through the patient's still
body.

'I've got a response!' Nicola exclaimed thankfully,
her stethoscope in place as soon as the paddles were
removed. 'Sinus rhythm. . .!'

CHAPTER THREE

THE bleep of the monitor confirmed Nicola's words and every member of the team smiled their relief at the reassuring sound.

No longer needed, Alys sped to the relatives' room to reassure the patient's wife. Finding her in tears, obviously dreading bad news, she draped a gently comforting arm about the bowed and shaking shoulders.

'Try not to worry, Mrs Marshall,' she said gently. 'The doctors have got his heart going and he'll probably be all right, thanks to your promptness in ringing for an ambulance.'

'It was all my fault, Sister!' She broke into fresh sobs. 'We'd had words and he got so angry and I knew his heart couldn't take it. But I was upset, too, and I just couldn't stop saying nasty things to him! I'll never forgive meself if he goes. . .'

'Heart attacks can happen without any provocation and you mustn't blame yourself,' Alys soothed. 'Everyone argues sometimes and I'm sure it was just coincidence that your husband was a little upset this morning.' She didn't bother to correct the misconception of her authority. Few people could differentiate between Sister and less senior nurses.

'Oh, do you really think so? He hasn't been well for

some days but he wouldn't see the doctor.' The poor woman clutched at straws. 'Can I see him, Sister?'

'Yes, in a few minutes, before he goes up to the cardiac unit. Then it might be a good idea for you to go home and get some rest. You aren't feeling very well yourself, are you?' Her experienced eye had detected the breathlessness of chronic emphysema.

'I've got me tablets, Sister.' She patted the bag in her capacious lap. 'Never go anywhere without them. When will they let Fred come home? He hates hospitals and I'm sure I can manage. . .'

'Well, not right away,' Alys cautioned, reluctant to raise false hopes. 'The doctors will want to do some tests and make sure there's no long-term damage and that could take a few weeks.' She got up from her uncomfortable perch on the arm of the chair. 'Would you like some more tea? That looks cold. And do let me know if there's someone I can telephone to come for you.'

'We're on our own since my son married and went to live abroad.' Mrs Marshall dabbed at her eyes with a wet hanky. 'But there's a neighbour — Mr Finn. He's ever so kind and he's got a car. He might come.' She rummaged in her handbag. 'I've got his number somewhere.'

Alys sent a junior for fresh tea for the relieved near-widow and made a call to the Marshalls' helpful neighbour. Then she hurried to the assistance of a schoolgirl who'd broken her wrist when she came off her bike but managed to reach A and E before collapsing from pain and shock.

So far that morning, neither Martin nor the SCO

had put in an appearance, and they seemed to be even busier than usual. She found herself glancing frequently at the outer doors in the hope that Zack would walk through them and scolded herself for a vague sense of disappointment when he didn't do so.

She was taking the vital signs of a woman found unconscious in a High Street store changing-room when Zack drew back the curtain. Alys caught her breath as she saw the dark bruise on his cheek and an unmistakable graze on his chin for she had seen enough combatants in Casualty to recognise all the signs of a fist fight.

His glance swept her so coldly that she cringed. 'I'm told that we have a problem with this patient, Staff,' he said with professional briskness, studying the grey-faced woman on the examining-couch.

Feeling strangely chilled, Alys handed him the chart. 'She arrived by ambulance some time ago and we can't rouse her although all the observations seem to be normal. She doesn't appear to be drunk and there's no indication of injury. The paramedics found aspirins as well as sleeping tablets in her handbag and suggest that she may have taken a couple from the wrong bottle by mistake to ease a bad headache. There's no indication that it was deliberate.'

'So we're just leaving her to sleep it off?'

His tone implied disapproval of Nicola's policy of non-action and Alys hastened to defend the overworked CO. 'We've been rushed off our feet this morning and her condition doesn't appear to be life-threatening. Dr Hastings decided not to call the neuro-surgical registrar until there are more definite signs of a real problem.' She added impulsively, 'What happened to your face, Zack?'

He put an involuntary hand to his cheek and winced as it came into contact with the tender flesh. 'You mean you don't know?' His tone was sardonic.

Alys looked at him in bewilderment. 'No. Should I?'

His eyes were stony. 'You might have warned me about your jealous boyfriend.'

'*Me!*' She squeaked in surprise. 'There must be some mistake. . .'

'Exactly what I said to Kemp when he accused me of setting you up for seduction,' he said grimly, wishing she had been more forthcoming about her romance with the CO. He had no desire to step on anyone's toes!

'You mean that *Martin* hit you!' Shock caused the blood to drain from her cheeks.

'He completely lost his cool but I'm sure he regrets it this morning. He's in much worse shape than I am.'

Alys was horrified, convinced that Martin's interference, however well-meant, had put paid to any hopes she might have cherished of becoming more than just another casualty nurse to Zachary Howes. It suddenly mattered very much that he should be disabused of the idea that Martin had any claim to her!

'I'm sorry. . . I don't know why he should do such a thing—I mean, he has no *right*!' she said helplessly. 'When did this happen?'

'Last night. I was on my way to my car after leaving you and he came charging at me like a madman.' Zack looked at her curiously. 'Don't you *know* when a man's obsessed with you, Alys?'

She blushed furiously. 'That's absurd! He's over-protective, that's all. . .'

'And he thinks you need protecting from me? Very flattering,' he said coldly.

Alys flinched from the cold steel of his deep-set eyes. 'Well, you do have a reputation for leading girls astray. . .' she joked, trying to lighten the moment, but she faltered to a halt at the abrupt hardening of his mouth.

Zack was rapidly losing patience with the gossips, and he was annoyed with his failure to resist her tug at his usually contained emotions. Falling in love with little miss innocence was no part of his plans for the future!

'I suggest you take what gossiping juniors say about me with a large pinch of salt and rely on your own judgement, Nurse Mackenzie,' he said coolly and bent over the unconscious patient, coiling strong fingers about a limp wrist and lifting the heavy eyelids to check the pupils. 'Some dilation and the pulse seems sluggish but if nothing abnormal is showing up then I think we can safely assume that the paramedics have got it right. But we'll admit her for twenty-four hours to be on the safe side. I'll organise a bed. . .'

He stalked from the cubicle in such high dudgeon that Alys wished she'd held her impulsive tongue. He probably thought she had exaggerated the events of that brief half-hour in his company to stir up Martin's emotions!

For the rest of the day, his distant manner hurt

much more than it ought and Wanda piled extra work on her shoulders, obviously knowing the cause of that contusion on Zack's cheek and punishing Alys for meeting him in Tommo's. Having been scolded for the slightest fault and assigned to the most awkward patients and most unpleasant jobs for the best part of the day, Alys thankfully took off her cap, unfastened her belt and put the towering bulk of St Benet's behind her that evening.

Standing at the bus stop, she saw the casualty sister crossing the road to the wine bar with Zack, and their smiling faces showed that they were friends again after a foolish quarrel that had led him to pay a brief, meaningless attention to her. Well, now he would probably drop the pretence that he found her attractive — and she could get on with her life without hankering for a man who didn't really want her at all, Alys told herself firmly.

She was slightly shocked that it had been so dangerously easy to want him. . .

On an impulse, she got off the bus before her usual stop to call on Martin, anxious to hear his version of that physical confrontation with Zachary Howes. As he opened the door of the elderly terraced house he was buying, she exclaimed in dismay. One eye was almost closed, his lip was split and his face was visibly bruised.

'Oh, Martin!' she said sadly. 'You came off worst, didn't you?'

He seemed unsurprised that she knew what had happened. 'Stupid, wasn't it?' He grimaced.

'*Unnecessary*, anyway,' she returned bluntly. She studied his marked face. 'It looks painful.'

'He's bigger than I am,' Martin reminded her with a smile that failed to conceal his burning resentment of the SCO.

'You can't possibly come to work until those bruises fade,' Alys said as he drew her into the house. 'Tongues *would* wag!'

'I can always say I was assaulted by a violent patient. It wouldn't be the first time,' he said wryly. 'But I suppose everyone knows that Zack and I had a punch-up?' He plugged in the kettle and took mugs from a wooden tree. 'Tea or coffee?'

'Anything. . .no, I don't think anyone knows except me—and Wanda, naturally. Now she *really* has a reason to make my life a misery—or thinks she has! Thanks a lot, Martin!'

'I'm sorry, Alys.'

'What did you think you were doing? Protecting me? I can look after myself perfectly well!' she said, a little crossly.

'I just saw red, I suppose. He only has to lift a finger and girls fall at his feet,' Martin said bitterly, thinking of Wanda rather than Alys. He was unexpectedly jealous, resenting her rapid recovery from losing him and her readiness to put Zack in his place. He had been content with the way things were between them until she spoiled their harmonious relationship by harping on marriage in spite of his warning that he wasn't the marrying kind, he thought bitterly. 'I've never liked the man and I don't like you liking him, even if it *isn't* any of my business.'

'I *don't* like him — not particularly.' Alys was trying to reassure herself as much as Martin.

'Did you make up your mind about that before or after you had a drink with him? I know you met him.'

It was irrefutable. 'I only wanted to know what prompted him to ask me,' she said defensively although she had no need to explain herself to Martin.

'And did you find out?'

'He was just getting back at Wanda for something she'd said or done to annoy him, I think.' Even to herself, Alys wouldn't admit the instinctive awareness that Zack found her attractive. 'But that doesn't excuse your hitting him, Martin. You must know what he thinks about us now!'

He poured boiling water on to the instant coffee grounds in both mugs. 'I'd like to think it was a matter of *us*, Alys,' he said deliberately. Refusing to regret the parting with Wanda, he was suddenly determined to prove his indifference and annoy Zack by dating the pretty and popular staff nurse.

'There must be better ways of telling me so than thumping Zachary Howes!' Her heart didn't miss a single beat for the words weren't totally unexpected. Martin ushered her into the untidy sitting-room and indicated the sofa before he plumped into a battered armchair. Cradling her mug of steaming coffee, Alys met the smile in his blue eyes with a little guilt although she hadn't encouraged him. 'I didn't know you felt that strongly,' she admitted ruefully.

Martin shrugged. 'You seem to keep men at arm's length. The "no time for romance" type. I felt you'd probably say no if I asked you for a date.'

'And then felt jealous because it seemed that I'd instantly said yes to Zack,' she said shrewdly.

'Everyone knows what he wants from a woman. I was afraid you'd fall for his line in chat-ups.'

Alys didn't want to believe that Zack's brief pursuit had been entirely sexual but the grapevine gossip made it hard to deny and an odd little lump of disappointment formed in her breast. 'You might credit me with more sense,' she said, all the more sharply because she had come close to falling for Zack's particular brand of charm. 'I'm not silly seventeen like some of the first-years who hang on his every word and almost swoon if he happens to smile at them.'

He leaned towards her with his own persuasive smile. 'I should have known he wouldn't sweet talk you into anything, Alys. You're too level-headed. Am I forgiven?'

His obvious concern for her eased the hurt of Zack's chilly and slightly scornful dismissal. Martin was very personable in spite of his fiery temper and Alys had always liked him. 'You should be apologising to Zack, not to me,' she told him sternly, but her eyes were soft.

He sighed. 'If that's what you want.'

'Make sure he knows that it was all a misunderstanding. I'm not your girlfriend, Martin,' she said firmly.

'Nor likely to be now, I suppose. I've really blotted my copybook.' Fingers interlaced about his coffee-mug, he stared into its contents.

He looked so dejected that Alys felt a tug at her tender heart. She mentally kicked herself even as she heard herself uttering the words that committed her to rather more than casual acquaintance. But there might be advantages to going out with Martin on occasions, she supposed. Wynne and Sally were always trying to pair her off with someone and she could cope with the easygoing young doctor who wasn't likely to make unwelcome demands on her emotions or try to hustle her into bed.

It would surely convince Zack that she was immune to his attractions, too. He seemed to be very angry with her at the moment but he might still like her enough to risk Wanda's displeasure and ask her out again one evening. And she might just be weak enough to say yes!

'Heavy day?' Wynne suggested as Alys fell into a convenient chair and reached for a reviving glass of wine in one fluid and speaking movement.

'Non-stop — and all the nasty ones, thanks to Sister Cas.' She cast a suspicious glance at the bottle of wine. 'Are we celebrating something?'

'A little bird told me you'd be dead on your feet and in need of some refreshment.'

'I suppose she also told you about Martin?'

'No. What's to tell?'

'Oh — nothing much.' Alys regretted the unthinking words as her friend's face brightened with eager interest. 'It was his day off.'

'Riveting news,' Wynne said sardonically.

She threw a handy cushion at her friend's dark head. 'And he isn't well,' she went on firmly. 'So I called to see him on my way home.'

'And. . .?'

'That's it. I thought I should mention it before the phone rings,' she said drily. 'I'm sure one of your little birds must have seen me knocking on his door and can't wait to report it!'

Wynne smiled sympathy, having suffered herself from a too efficient grapevine in the past. 'What's wrong with Martin?'

'Just a bug of sorts,' Alys said evasively. 'He's taking the rest of the week off to get over it.'

'And you've volunteered to nurse him?'

'You live in hope, don't you?' Alys teased.

'You could do worse. He's a nice lad, is Martin. . . and he likes you a lot, Alys. You should snap him up!' Wynne's advice was automatic for she had long since given up trying to matchmake for her stubbornly unattached friend.

'Perhaps I have. . .' She smiled into her glass of wine as Wynne's face registered disbelief. 'He's taking me to the charity ball on Saturday.' Alys surreptitiously crossed her fingers on the unspoken hope that Martin's black eye and various bruises would have faded by the weekend, giving the juniors less to talk about. 'Will you fix the hem on my new dress, Wynne? It needs shortening.'

'How can I refuse when Cinderella's actually made a date with Prince Charming at last?'

Alys wrinkled her nose. 'Would you say Prince Charming? More like Dandini, don't you think?'

'Dandini doesn't get the girl,' Wynne reminded her sternly. 'Frankly, I've always thought him a safer bet than his boss. I never could understand why Cinders preferred the prince.'

This particular Cinders meant to do all she could to keep from preferring the prince, Alys told herself sensibly as she ran a hot bath to ease out the stresses and strains of the day.

Zachary Howes was a charmer with a smile that quickened her pulses but she knew all the dangers of liking him too much. Martin was a much more reliable choice if she was tempted to relent and allow someone into the heart she had kept on hold for so long.

Alys felt she had good reason to be wary of allowing her heart to rule her head. Her mother had been a ward sister at St Benet's before she fell in love and rushed into a marriage that hadn't survived the contrasting dullness of life as the wife of a country GP. Badly affected by the marital discord and eventual divorce of her parents, inclined to distrust the powerful emotions that could sweep totally unsuited people into marriage, Alys was determined not to make the mistake of loving the wrong man.

Her mother's nostalgia for the happy years at Benny's had inspired her to follow in her footsteps and train as a nurse and her father had promised her a job with his practice when she qualified. However, long before she proudly pinned her silver badge of a St Benet's nurse to the bib of her apron, he had sold his practice and gone to South Africa with a new wife.

Alys had never quite forgiven her adored father for walking out of her life and as a result she hesitated to give her heart to any man who might let her down as he had done. She would need to be very, very sure that any man to whom she eventually gave her heart could be trusted with her happiness.

Which probably ruled out Zachary Howes, for a start. . .

CHAPTER FOUR

THE alarming bleep of a monitor sent Alys hurrying back to the cubicle she had briefly left. The occupant had walked into A and E that morning, complaining of crushing chest pains and difficulty in breathing, signs of an imminent myocardial infarction. Zack had immediately given him an injection to ease his discomfort and ordered X-rays and an electrocardiograph, and the young man had been left to rest while a bed was found for him in the cardiac unit.

First on the scene, Alys sent a junior nurse scurrying for the SCO and began to resuscitate the patient, placing her hands firmly on the ominously still chest and pressing down hard in an attempt to restart the reluctant heart, interrupting the rhythm only long enough to cover the patient's mouth with her own to force air into the flaccid lungs.

'All right, Alys. . .' Zack took over as he arrived at her side, followed by the alerted crash team, and she stepped aside, her own heart beating alarmingly fast with the surge of adrenalin that always accompanied a sudden emergency.

The crash trolley was pushed into place and the heavy defibrillator plugged in, jelly pads placed on the man's chest in preparation for the charge and monitor leads moved around for synchronisation while the

anaesthetist injected life-saving drugs into the cannula
that Alys had set up earlier.

'Two hundred joules. . .' Zack instructed quietly.

The assisting physician waited for the needle to
climb to the required figure and then released the
charge. The man's powerful body jerked and the
percussive sound hung in the air. The monitor screen
showed no reaction.

Zack didn't hesitate. 'Four hundred joules!'

The procedure was repeated but even that powerful
charge of electricity couldn't kick start the heart. The
team continued their efforts for some considerable
time although it was obvious to everyone that it was a
lost cause.

Near to tears, Alys left the cubicle, blaming herself
for not staying with a patient who might not have died
if she had been on the spot to notice the danger signs
of cardiac distress.

Four years of nursing had often shown her the
darker side of medicine but she hated losing patients
and she grieved for this one who had seemed so strong
and fit, so full of life, talking about his job and the
sports he loved and the girlfriend who had just begun
to train as a Benny's nurse.

Like so many patients, he had confided to her
sympathetic ear the anxiety he hadn't admitted to the
doctors and she had promised him that he had nothing
to worry about. Now, those assurances echoed emptily
in her ears and the ache in her throat was accompanied
by the sting of tears.

The office was empty and she sat down at the desk,
resting her head on her arms, crying for a stranger and

all the dreams he had known that would never now come true. Perhaps, deep down, she cried for her own unadmitted dreams, too. . .

'Hey! What's this?' Zack crouched beside her chair, his voice soft and concerned. As she raised a wet face from her folded arms, he tenderly thumbed the welling tears from her cheeks.

'I shouldn't have left him alone. . .' With an effort, Alys swallowed the huge lump in her throat and fought back the tears.

'We'd eased his pain and stabilised him. With plenty of staff on hand, there was no reason for you to special him,' he soothed. 'Particularly as we're having such a busy morning.'

His smile was so kind and understanding that she almost laid her head on his chest and sobbed anew. All her emotions were dangerously near the surface of late, she realised in dismay. 'I didn't feel happy about him. There was something, a look about him — I don't know.' How could she describe a gut feeling that many nurses experienced after years of working on the wards? 'I meant to go back to check on him and then I heard the blip and knew it was too late. . .'

'You did what you could, Alys. We all did.'

'Yes, I know.' She managed a watery smile. 'Sorry. I'm being over-emotional. Forgetting that I'm a nurse. But I can't help feeling that he died needlessly. Nurse Crisp called me to help with a nosebleed. For something so trivial, a man died——' She broke off, biting her lip.

'There was nothing we could do to restart his heart — and God knows we tried.'

'Yes. . .' She saw in his sombre eyes that the death of any patient hurt him, too. Moved by his pain, she impulsively laid her hand along the cheek that still bore a slight graze. 'I'm so sorry about that, Zack,' she said on an impulsive rush of regret. He was so much nicer than she had known and she was sure that Martin had spoiled what might have been a beautiful friendship.

He turned his head to nibble her fingers with his lips, meaning to lighten the moment, but her heart missed a beat at the brush of his warm mouth and she jerked her hand away in sudden, fierce alarm that he read as rejection.

Disappointment was reflected in his eyes but he said nothing, straightening up as a first-year put her head round the door, fortunately too agitated to notice anything amiss or A and E would be buzzing with more rumours, he thought drily.

'Staff, can you come?'

Alys leaped up at the agonised note of urgency in the girl's voice. 'Right away. . .' She welcomed the interruption, shaken to the core of her being by a glimpse of what it must be like to be loved by someone as caring as Zachary Howes. No wonder Sister Cas had laid claim to him and meant to hold on to him with both hands while she decided whether or not to marry him. . .

An ancient alcoholic had been found crumpled in a doorway by a passing policeman who had recognised that the man was ill rather than drunk. Alys followed the anxious first-year into the cubicle where the elderly patient, shabby and unmistakably smelly, was curled up in the foetal position on the examining-couch.

'What's the problem?' she asked, automatically checking the vital signs, observing the sluggish pulse and the fixed and dilated pupils.

'He's dead, isn't he, Staff?'

Nurse Ramsay was very young and visibly overwhelmed by her first experience of casualty work and Alys suspected that the girl had never come face to face with death. She looked distressed and her hands trembled as she mopped at the slack mouth and grey, sunken cheeks, needing to appear to be doing something for the patient although she was much too inexperienced even to know that he wasn't dead at all.

'No. He's in coma. He may have had a stroke or be suffering the results of a head injury or he may simply be diabetic, in which case we shall need to give him an injection of insulin. Go and ask Dr Howes to come and look at him, Nurse.'

Zack arrived within moments, tall and broad and reassuring, the junior fluttering helplessly in his wake. Alys had checked the blood-pressure and found it dangerously high and she had no hesitation in making a snap diagnosis. 'He's showing all the signs of a cerebral bleed,' she announced.

'Has anyone suggested a CAT scan?'

'No. He only came in fifteen minutes ago and Nurse was still cleaning him up. He was in a pretty filthy state, I'm afraid.'

'Still is,' Zack said drily, backing slightly from the stench of unwashed humanity. 'Right, I'll arrange for the scan if you'll contact John Winter in the neurosurgical unit. He might need to drill a couple of burr holes in the skull to relieve pressure on the brain once the bleeding area shows up. . .'

With a soft, sighing moan, the junior nurse slumped against him and the unsurprised SCO caught hold of her, supporting her with strong arms. 'We appear to have another casualty, Staff,' he said with a glimmer of a smile.

'It's her first day and I think she's finding it all too much for her,' Alys said, hastily putting her own arms about the unconscious girl.

He looked down at the pale, very youthful face beneath the awry cap. 'She's just a child,' he said sympathetically.

'Straight from training school,' Alys agreed. 'It happens to us all at one time or another. I fainted on my first day in Theatre.'

'I gather that's almost obligatory.'

Still smarting from her involuntary rejection of a tender overture, he was a little dismayed that a persistent desire for the pretty Alys Mackenzie was overcoming his ability to handle her cautious attitude. More than Kemp stood in his way, he knew. He needed to convince her that he was to be trusted and wanted her happiness as much as his own — and that meant undoing the harm done by a past and much regretted reputation as a Romeo. They needed to talk — and soon. . .

But, in the meantime, there was work to be done and a squeamish student nurse to be brought round and comforted. Between them, they got the girl into a chair. As soon as she regained consciousness, she burst into tears, and Alys dispatched her in the care of another nurse to the rest-room.

Later in the day, Zack snatched a moment to ask about the young nurse. 'Much better,' Alys assured him, smiling her appreciation of his concern. 'She insisted on coming back to work although Wanda said she could report sick. How's our man with the head injury?'

'He's in Theatre. . .the scan showed a ruptured aneurysm and John Winter decided on immediate surgery. Hopefully, he'll do. . .' He used the usual term for those patients expected to make a full recovery from accident or sudden illness.

The friendliness in his grey eyes and the curve of his warm mouth was encouraging and she knew she was forgiven for that forceful rebuff. As they had to work together, it was good to feel that they could be friends. But she really didn't want anything more than that for liking Zachary Howes too much would only complicate her life and her job—and she had no intention of competing with Wanda Nelson for the SCO!

Moving on, Zack paused for a brief word with Nicola. Hearing his attractive laugh, Alys turned to see them with their heads together in a shared joke. The hard-working CO was never too busy to respond to his smiling charm and he seemed unable to resist a little mild flirtation with any attractive girl who crossed his path, Alys thought with a little stab of irritation. Thank heavens she had too much sense to take anything he said or did as a serious sign of intent or interest!

'We were just talking about the charity ball,' Nicola

confided as she came into the cubicle where Alys was comforting a patient with severe stomach pains. 'Unfortunately, I'm on duty, but I hope to look in for an hour or so and Zack's promised to save me a dance. Are you going?' Without waiting for a reply, she bent over the groaning woman on the couch. 'Can you tell me about your pain, Mrs Mason? Is it bad here? Or here?' Practised hands gently pressed and probed the tender abdomen. 'It may be your appendix that's causing the problem. I think we'll ask the surgical registrar to take a look at you. . .'

Alys had agreed that Martin should take her to the midsummer charity ball, an annual event organised by the Friends of St Benet's Hospital, having turned down both a persistent medical student and an admiring paramedic who found it hard to accept that she just wasn't interested in romance.

They called her cold and perhaps she would believe it if she hadn't experienced that tingling excitement at Zack's touch. But the feelings he evoked were possibly the first steps on the slippery slope of heartache and disillusion and no doubt she was safer with someone like Martin.

Dancing with him in the crowded ballroom, the layered frills of her scarlet Spanish-style dress swishing about her knees and a matching Spanish comb complementing her upswept curls, she looked over his shoulder and directly into Zack's enigmatic eyes as he danced past them with Wanda, who had made sure the whole world knew he was taking her to the midsummer ball.

As it was *the* romantic event of the hospital calendar

there had been much speculation that the SCO and
Sister Cas meant to announce their engagement that
night and Wanda's confident clutch at Zack's arm as
they crossed the ballroom on arrival, followed by the
way she linked her arms about his neck and smiled
into his eyes as they danced, seemed to support the
rumour.

Alys couldn't help wondering if he'd used all his
considerable powers of persuasion to convince her that
marrying him wasn't such a bad idea, after all.

Well, she wished them luck, she thought with an
odd stir of defiance.

Disconcerted by the way her heart had leapt as she
met Zack's gaze, she threw back her head to smile up
at Martin with a warmth intended to deceive the SCO
and anyone else who might be watching about their
relationship.

People began to drift from the dance-floor as the
music came to a brief halt and she nodded at the
lovingly entwined couple who made their way to the
table near their own. 'Don't forget your promise,' she
said sternly, reminding Martin of the deal they had
made when she agreed to go to the ball with him.

He stiffened. 'You really want me to apologise for
hitting him!' In the intervening days, Martin had hoped
that *she* would forget.

'You've got to face him eventually and A and E isn't
the ideal place to sort out your differences.' Alys
smiled at him encouragingly. 'You did get it all wrong,
Martin. Surely you only have to look at him with
Wanda to realise that!'

With an inexplicable heaviness about her heart, she

felt that everyone at the ball that night must share her conviction that the couple were on the verge of matrimony, as the juniors declared. It was one rumour that couldn't easily be dismissed, not like the many others about his flirtatious tendencies that she was inclined to doubt.

Swallowing his pride to please her, Martin reached to touch the SCO's broad shoulder. 'Apparently I owe you an apology.' Tone and manner were curt, ungracious. 'I was out of order the other evening. No hard feelings, I hope?'

Zack looked beyond the CO to the girl who hovered with a half-smile lighting her pretty face. He suspected that Kemp wouldn't be apologising if she hadn't urged him to do so in return for her favours and he felt a fierce, all-consuming jealousy.

'We all make mistakes,' he said coolly. 'Forget it. . .' He turned away with his arm about Wanda, who had been visibly upset to see Kemp and Alys together, parading their closeness. Zack had made light of it to comfort her but now he felt just as sick at heart with the realisation that the staff nurse must be more involved with the man than he had dreamed.

Martin shrugged. 'At least I tried,' he said defensively as he urged Alys through the cluster of tables surrounding the dance-floor.

Wisely, she said nothing, but she couldn't blame Zack for rejecting that obviously insincere apology. Perhaps she should have left them to settle the matter in their own way and in their own time. . .

She stole several wistful glances at the man who was so relaxed in the company of his friends, handsome face alight with laughter at the merry crosstalk, and felt a foolish envy of the girl who seemed so sure of his love and could look forward to spending the rest of her life with him.

Unaware that her expressive face betrayed her, she was surprised when Zack approached to ask her to dance. She hesitated, glancing at Martin for approval, a fact that didn't escape Zack. But the hot-tempered CO was caught up in an argument about trust hospitals and private medicine and appeared not to notice as she smiled at Zack and got to her feet.

The band was playing the lambada, very suited to her vivid dress, but Alys was wary as his arms went round her, knowing the blatant sensuality of the dance and her own disturbing reaction to the closeness of his powerful frame. She relaxed as he looked down at her with a reassuring warmth in his smile and suddenly she laughed up at him, hazel eyes dancing with mischief.

'Taking a chance, aren't you?' she teased.

He laughed, understanding. 'Risking another assault by your boyfriend, do you mean?'

'Risking excommunication by your girlfriend!' she amended, with a meaningful glance at the disapproving casualty sister, wondering why Zack wanted to incite jealousy and stir up gossip by singling her out. Somehow, it seemed unlikely behaviour for a man who was about to announce his engagement, she felt with a sudden lift of her spirits.

'You've got it wrong, Alys. Wanda and I are just good friends,' Zack said lightly. It was no less than the truth and he might have clarified matters if Alys had instantly denied that Kemp was a serious contender for her affections. As the man obviously meant a great deal to her, there was no point.

Alys greeted the hackneyed phrase with a cynical smile. 'You could say the same for Martin and me,' she returned, thinking that it was perfectly true in *their* case.

A frown formed in the deep-set eyes and his arms tightened about her abruptly. 'Let's forget both of them for a few minutes,' he suggested softly, sensing a yielding as she relaxed against him, and wondering if she realised the passion that leaped to life as he held her.

The seductive sensuality of the dance demanded all her concentration for the next few minutes. Zack danced well, his powerful but fluid body moving in perfect rhythm with her own. Her heart raced as his arms held her close and his cheek pressed against her clustered curls. There was a fluttering of imprisoned butterflies in the pit of her stomach and her legs felt so trembly that it was not only the sway and the pace of the dance that made it necessary for her to cling so tightly to his broad shoulder.

Breathless, she was laughing and radiant as the music ended and he swung her round in his arms. 'Oh, I enjoyed that!' she exclaimed ingenuously.

Zack only just stopped himself from kissing her. 'So did I. . .' He drew her into another dance as the band struck up a foxtrot. He smiled down at her and crooned the words of the old love song that the band played.

Alys suppressed the leap of her heart. 'Don't flirt with me, Zack. I can't take any more of Wanda's little punishments,' she said lightly, reminding herself that he *was* only flirting with her and it was foolish to take anything he said or did for real.

He smiled. 'She does delight in making things tough for you, I've noticed. But I'm not taking responsibility for that, Alys. She had you jumping through hoops long before I made the mistake of seeing you as something more than just another well-trained robot in a nurse's uniform.'

It was reckless, probably dangerous, but Alys looked up at him with a dance of mischief in her hazel eyes. '*Was* it such a mistake?' she murmured, softly, provocatively.

His eyes were warm as they looked into her own, causing a *frisson* of excitement. 'Don't *you* flirt with *me*, Alys. I can't take any more temptation without doing something about it,' he warned with a drawl in his deep voice that sent a shock of delight along her spine and tingling all the way to her toes.

His arms held her close and he twined long fingers in the curls that escaped from the Spanish comb to nestle on her nape and bent his handsome head to nuzzle her soft neck like a lover. . .

CHAPTER FIVE

THE tang of Zack's aftershave mingling with the male scent of him and the delicious promise in his touch and his kiss stirred Alys almost unbearably as they danced.

The weakness of wanting him so much shocked and alarmed her slightly but she was past caring as they moved together to the lilting music, locked in that exciting embrace and concealed from watchful eyes by the press of the dancers about them.

In the midst of delight, Alys wondered bleakly if he would be so careless with his light kisses and the caress of his strong hands on her back and shoulders if he thought that Wanda could see them from the other side of the huge ballroom.

Zack struggled with the fierce, insistent throb of desire that she triggered with her sweet, soft femininity. It bothered him that he couldn't dismiss the longing for a girl who was apparently committed to another man. Both Alys and Kemp were making it crystal-clear that they were a couple and it did no good to go on wanting her so much. The trouble was that he simply couldn't stop!

He longed to transport her to another place, far from Wanda and Kemp and the rest of the world, if only for one brief hour of happiness in her arms.

Deep down, he suspected that he would want that dream to go on forever. . .

'When are you having dinner with me?' he asked, smiling into her beautiful eyes as they made their way back to their respective tables.

'I'm not,' Alys returned brightly, steeling her resistance to his insidious charm. 'Wanda wouldn't approve!' With a laughing toss of her head and a flounce of her frilly skirts, she left him and resumed her seat beside Martin in a flurry of heightened senses that made her thankful she'd turned down the temptation of that look in Zack's eyes and the invitation offered in his deep, thrilling voice.

He had a powerful physical magnetism that made a girl want to throw caution to the wind and lose herself — and perhaps her heart — in his strong arms. But she mustn't allow it to happen, she warned herself sternly as she watched him slip an arm about the lovely girl in the simple black dress that made her own striking outfit seem flamboyant.

She saw Wanda lean back against Zack's broad and welcoming shoulder, flirting an answering smile, so sure of him that Alys felt as if a cruel hand suddenly squeezed her heart. Until he made it clear just how involved he was with the casualty sister, she had no intention of showing how much *she* liked and wanted him.

On a surge of pride, she turned her back on the couple and linked her hand in Martin's arm. He smiled at her with a flattering warmth and no hint of reproach because she had leaped up so eagerly to dance with the SCO.

'Let's dance, Martin,' she said impulsively and within moments they were on the dance-floor, her laughing enjoyment meant to show Zachary Howes that those moments in his arms were already forgotten.

Perhaps it wasn't fair to mislead Martin but she thought she could trust him not to put unwelcome pressure on her and she meant to stop dating him the moment she felt he was in danger of being hurt. Fortunately, he was a very different man from the sensual SCO who probably hustled a girl into bed at the first sign of weakening resistance to his potent persuasions, if the juniors could be believed, and she was grateful that Martin asked so little of her while providing her with a smokescreen for the foolish longing for another man.

If she was so ripe for falling in love, then surely Martin was a better recipient of her hopes and dreams than someone who seemed seriously committed to Wanda Nelson in spite of the glow in his grey eyes and the thrill of his feather-light lips on her face and hair, the promise in his powerful body as he held her close in the movements of the dance.

Only a fool who didn't care what happened to her heart would believe that he meant anything by those sense-stirring attentions. . .

Plastering was an unpopular and time-consuming chore but Alys did her best to make it as painless as possible for the eleven-year-old who had crashed his new mountain bike into a garden wall. He was as stoical as most boys of his age, more concerned for his damaged bike than himself, and anxious to know if he could skip school while his arm was mending.

'I'm afraid not, Jeremy.' She broke the bad news

gently as she smoothed wet plaster of Paris over the Colles' fracture. 'Luckily, you're right-handed, and it's the left wrist that's broken so you'll have no problems with your written work.' She saw from his crestfallen face that she had said the wrong thing and gave him a sympathetic hug.

'Need any help with that, Alys?' Martin put his fair head through the cubicle curtains. 'Rush-hour approaches. . .'

'Almost finished. A few more minutes. . .'

'Looks as if you fell off *your* bike,' Jeremy said with the blunt cheerfulness of the pre-teen schoolboy, keen eyes noting the not-quite-faded discoloration of a recent black eye.

Martin grinned. 'Something like that,' he agreed good-naturedly, but he was sensitive about the hammering he'd received at Zack's powerful hands. It had been only a couple of blows but they'd done a fair amount of damage, more to his pride than his face.

One more reason to detest a man who seemed to possess the Midas touch, succeeding in anything that he attempted, securing good jobs because of a natural brilliance with which no amount of studying and striving by lesser men could compete, and winning the affections of women without visible effort, Martin thought bitterly. If an opportunity offered itself to get back at him in some way he would seize it with both hands and damn the consequences!

In the meantime, dating a girl that Howes unmistakably found attractive gave him a satisfactory buzz of revenge for past rivalries and maybe assured Wanda

that he had no regrets about breaking with her even if
it wasn't strictly true. . .

Having finished her task of plastering the schoolboy's injured wrist, Alys hurried to help where she
could for mid-morning was a particularly busy time in
A and E when half the population had falls or crashed
cars or suffered heart attacks or decided that an ankle
sprained days earlier needed urgent hospital attention.

Children fell off swings and expectant mums went
into early labour in street or supermarket and work-
men fell on their tools. Pensioners who hadn't eaten
properly for weeks keeled over and toddlers tormented
the family pet until they were bitten or scratched,
drank from bottles that contained anything but lem-
onade or ate handfuls of toxic 'sweeties' that should
have been kept in a safe place.

'Another pair of hands might be a useful Christmas
present,' Alys murmured to Martin later that morning
as she wheeled one old lady with a suspected hip
fracture towards the X-ray department while reassuring another who clutched at her arm, demanding
instant attention for an already bandaged hand.

He grinned. 'I'll bear it in mind,' he promised over
his shoulder as he steered an elderly gentleman
towards Reception.

Alys realised that he was taking it for granted that
they would be together when Christmas came around,
several months away. Junior nurses were already call-
ing them a couple and somehow, without meaning to,
it seemed that she had drifted into a relationship that
only she refused to regard as a promising romance.

The charity ball had a lot to answer for, she thought wryly.

Zack put his dark head through the gap in a cubicle curtain. 'Spare a minute, Staff!'

His patient was ashen-faced, eyes dark-ringed and dilated, mouth stained black by charcoal. Having undergone the unpleasantness of a stomach wash-out, the girl looked very sorry for herself but it seemed to a surprised Alys that Zack had little sympathy for someone who had overdosed on a mix of pain-killers and vodka in a deliberate suicide attempt.

She gently smoothed the sweat-darkened hair and wiped the bloodless lips, her tender heart torn by such obvious distress. 'I know you must be feeling awful but we'll do our best to make you more comfortable,' she soothed, hoping the girl felt grateful for being snatched from the death she had apparently desired, if only at a moment of madness.

For answer, she groaned and vomited into a kidney dish, and Alys took a handful of tissues to clean her up. The teenager lay back with closed eyes, stupefied by the combination of drugs and alcohol she had absorbed into her system.

'Do we know *why*?' Alys ventured to ask, turning to the frowning physician.

Zack looked up from the notes that would accompany the girl to a ward where she would be closely observed for a day or two. 'Broke up with her boyfriend,' he said curtly. 'There's no history of mental problems but I'm recommending a pyschiatric assessment. She's very lucky that her flatmate felt uneasy and turned back after leaving for work and then had the presence of mind to call an ambulance.'

'She must have been feeling very unhappy.'

'She feels worse now. Maybe she'll think twice before attempting it again,' Zack said bluntly and the patient stirred uneasily as the harsh words penetrated her cloudy mind.

'People in love aren't rational at such times,' Alys defended, surprised and disappointed by his tone with its apparent lack of compassion. 'I expect it was done on impulse — the "I'll make him sorry" syndrome. She'll probably never do it again.'

He met the reproach in her eyes with steel in his own. 'Make sure she knows that she ran the risk of severe brain damage or being on dialysis for the rest of her life. People who take overdoses are more likely to become a burden to themselves and their families than to succeed in ending it all.'

Tears gathered in the girl's dilated eyes in response to the scathing censure. Alys bent over her with a soothing touch and smile, wishing she had the authority to rebuke Zack for being so unfeeling. As she pushed the fall of tangled red hair from the pale face, the patient winced.

'That hurts, does it?' Alys queried, seeing a raised and reddened bump on the girl's brow. She drew Zack's attention to the bruise. 'It looks as if Sandra may have hit her head on something when she collapsed.'

Cool, clever fingers explored the sensitive area. 'We'll check it out,' he decided. 'I'll order an X-ray. . .'

Alys followed him to the central desk, a militancy in her hazel eyes. 'You were unnecessarily hard on that poor girl,' she accused, breaking the cardinal rule that nurses did not challenge doctors. 'Did you have to be so unkind when she could hear every word you said?'

'I doubt if anything I said registered very clearly, more's the pity. I've no time for cowards, Alys. Living may not always be easy but dying too young is a damn sight harder and I get angry when I see kids like that one overdosing for no good reason,' he told her bluntly, taking an X-ray request form from a pigeon-hole and uncapping his pen.

'A broken romance can seem an excellent reason to a seventeen-year-old. I thought you had more heart!' Disappointment sharpened her tone. 'It seems that I don't know you very well at all!'

'That could be remedied if you gave me half a chance,' he suggested with a sudden smile, admiring the spirited animation in her pretty face.

'Working here gives us both more than half a chance to get to know each other but it can obviously be deceptive,' she countered, ignoring the flattering warmth of words that seemed to sweep aside her concern. 'You're not the caring, compassionate person I thought you were!'

Zack's warm mouth hardened into a cold, uncompromising line. 'I keep my compassion for those who merit it, Staff. Now, I expect you have some work to do?'

Suddenly, there was no trace of warm friendliness in his eyes and the deep voice that could quicken her heartbeats with its tender tones sounded cold and unfriendly. Alys stalked away from him to study the board with its chalked list of patients and problems that needed attention, culled by the reception clerks on arrival, seeing it through a haze of angry dismay.

Maybe sympathy was the last thing that should be applied in such a case and maybe Zack's anger was meant to make an overwrought teenager realise the irresponsibility of her reaction to an emotional upset. But his harshness made no allowance for the intensity of young love!

Had he never gone through it himself? Had he never known the joys and despairs, the hopes and disappointed dreams, the mood swings and giddy roundabouts of love? Alys was only just beginning to understand it for herself but as Wanda had refused to marry Zack, even if she had since changed her mind, surely *he* could sympathise with someone who had loved and lost!

Still smarting from his dismissive tone, she was in the right frame of mind to cope with a diabetic patient who had missed his insulin and enjoyed a liquid lunch with disastrous results.

Fighting drunk, he forcibly resisted the insulin that was essential to restore the alkali balance in his blood before he went into coma. It wasn't the first time that the same man had been brought into A and E in a similar state, wasting the time and resources of busy nurses through self-neglect.

Ignoring the stream of abuse, overcoming his objection with her determined stance, Alys gave the injection, warning him again of the dangers of ignoring his need for insulin and indulging his liking for alcohol.

As reason returned, he slurred an apology, 'Bloody nuisance, that's me, eh, nurse? Got better things to do than straighten me out, haven't you?'

He beamed at her as if they were old friends — and so they were in a way for she was getting to know the regulars after nearly two months in the department. 'I won't argue with you on that score,' she said in dry agreement, a little breathless and slightly bruised from the struggle.

Alerted by the disturbance, Zack strode into the cubicle, somewhat surprised that the usually solicitous Kemp hadn't already rushed to her aid.

'Need some help, Staff?'

'I can manage, thank you, Doctor,' Alys said coolly, his criticism of her still rankling.

The patient clutched at Zack's arm to detain him as he turned to leave. 'This nurse says I'm a bloody nuisance, Doc. I object to that! Got a right to treatment like everyone else, haven't I? I resent being called a bloody nuisance. I'm a sick man. . .'

The man's whining tone won him no sympathy from Zack. 'You wouldn't be so sick if you remembered your insulin and kept off the whisky, Arthur,' he said sternly, unconsciously echoing Alys. 'We're seeing far too much of you here. Please make this the last time.' He glanced through the notes. 'Stay on that couch and I'll look in on you later.' On his way from the cubicle, he summoned Alys with an imperative jerk of his head. 'Staff, I want you. . .'

Used to the unconscious arrogance of senior doctors, Alys followed him. In agreement with the hard line he had taken this time, she was unprepared for the chilly disapproval in his unsmiling eyes as she looked up at him, waiting for instructions.

With her hands clasped demurely behind her back and a suitably attentive expression in her hazel eyes, she looked so much the part of well-trained nurse and so appealingly pretty in her light blue dress and pert cap that Zack almost forgot to be cross with her. He steeled himself to call her to task.

'I'm very disappointed in your attitude, Alys,' he told her bluntly. 'If you don't control that impulsive tongue you'll find yourself on report.'

She stared in surprise at the slap of the words. 'Now what have I done?' she asked blankly.

Zack hardened his heart. 'I know that some patients can be difficult and offensive but you've been a nurse long enough to know that it's an occupational hazard. There's no excuse for name-calling, whatever the provocation. Don't do it again,' he said sternly.

'Name-calling. . .!' Alys spluttered with indignation. 'You've got it all wrong! If there was any abuse flying about it certainly wasn't coming from me!' She smarted at the unjust accusation, recalling the stream of ugly abuse as she injected the insulin.

'Mr Burrows obviously feels that he has a grievance and I wouldn't have said that he was the over-sensitive type,' Zack said drily.

'I didn't call the man a nuisance, bloody or otherwise!' she flared with uncharacteristic anger, incensed by the injustice of the accusation. 'They were *his* words, not mine — and I'm amazed that you're so ready to believe his version of what was said! Not to mention making a mountain out of a molehill!' She was furious, hazel eyes blazing. 'You're being bloody unreasonable — and if *that's* name-calling then go ahead and put me on report for it!'

He turned on his heel, smouldering, and the passing Nicola paused to raise an eyebrow at his bristling back as he strode from that sharp exchange with the usually sweet-tempered staff nurse.

'What was that all about? Zack doesn't seem too pleased with you,' she sympathised.

Alys shrugged. 'I'm not very pleased with him at the moment,' she retorted tartly. 'Bloody arrogant doctors!'

Nicola smiled. 'I can only apologise for my colleague. We all tend to take it out on the poor nurses when things aren't going well, I'm afraid.'

Calming down, Alys smiled back at the CO whose days were long and tiring and much more demanding than her own. 'I think he's having a bad day,' she relented, although Zack didn't deserve her support. 'He was quite callous about that OD.'

'It *is* a bad day for him, actually,' Nicola said quietly. 'And that was the last thing he needed, today of all days.' Alys shot her a puzzled glance and the CO went on, 'He isn't saying much but I was at university with Jenny Howes and I know how he must be feeling.'

Alys was startled. 'His wife. . .?'

'His sister. I thought you knew about Jenny. . .she died four years ago today. Zack can't help but have it on his mind, I'm sure. She was only nineteen and a brilliant student. Such a waste. . .'

'Do you mean she took an overdose?' Her eyes widened in dismay. 'Oh, how dreadful!'

'Heavens, no!' Nicola hastened to put right a false impression. 'Jenny had an inoperable cerebral tumour. She had medical treatment, including a course of chemotherapy, but she died within four months of diagnosis——'

She broke off as Alys hurried away in obvious pursuit of the SCO and the caution that Nicola had meant to add, knowing Zack's fierce pride, remained unsaid. . .

CHAPTER SIX

ALYS tracked Zack to the emergency-room and he turned from removing X-ray plates from the rack and sliding them into protective covers, arcing a dark eyebrow at her breathless entry.

'Zack! I'm so sorry! I've just heard about your sister. . .' She stopped short as the initial impetus of impulse ground to a halt before his discouraging expression. 'I've been horrid to you all day, too,' she finished lamely, a delicate flush tinging her cheeks.

'Have you? I've been too busy to notice.' Zack continued to study an illumined X-ray plate as if it was vital to absorb its information, resisting the urge to sweep her into his arms and find comfort for a lingering sense of loss in the sweetness of her lips.

His absent tone rebuffed her warm-hearted contrition and Alys regretted the impulse that had hurtled her into a suddenly embarrassing situation.

Studying his broad, uncompromising back, she felt a sudden, startling shock of wanting—a wanting that she must learn to conquer and conceal, for his effect on her emotions had nothing whatsoever to do with loving, she told herself sternly. Zack might promise an excitement and an ecstasy she had never found in any other man's arms but the protective ice about her heart was still intact. . .

'I really am sorry, Zack,' she went on bravely. 'If

I'd known what today meant to you, I wouldn't have accused you of being uncaring about that OD.'

She sounded so contrite that Zack softened. He glanced over his shoulder with a hint of a smile lightening his expression. 'I intended to tell you about Jenny—and a few other things—the night we met in Tommo's. Over a leisurely dinner. But you took fright and ran away.'

'I *didn't* run away!' Alys denied instantly, indignation sparking. 'I'd already made plans. . .'

'To meet Kemp? Is that why he attacked me?' He turned to look at her with challenging grey eyes. 'Why didn't you tell me that night that you were involved with him?'

'Because I *wasn't*—then!'

'But you are now.'

Her chin shot up in resentment. He was involved with Wanda, wasn't he? How dared he reproach her for dating another man. 'I've known Martin for some time,' she said evasively.

'And it's serious, is it?'

She smiled the feminine, infuriating smile of a woman who meant to keep her own counsel. 'Maybe. . .'

Zack sighed. 'I expected better than that from you, Alys,' he deplored. 'A straight answer, for instance.'

'You've no right to be asking the questions!' she said crisply. 'And I've work to do. . .' She turned to the door but he leaned across to snap it shut and set a hand on either side of her so that her slight frame was trapped between the door and his powerful body, his unsmiling face only inches from her own.

'I've no right to kiss you, either,' he said tensely, and did so.

His mouth was surprisingly gentle, his kiss full of a magical promise that caused her head to swim and her legs to weaken. Alys fought the temptation to cling to him for support, knowing she should be pushing him away instead of kissing him back, warming to his ardent possession of her lips with an eager excitement coursing through her veins.

The man was an enigma, she sighed. How was a girl supposed to know if he was or wasn't in love with the casualty sister when he didn't make his intentions clear by word or behaviour? *Was* he only flirting when he smiled at *her* with that irresistible charm or did he mean the tender longing that she sometimes glimpsed in his eyes? And had he been genuiunely disappointed when she turned aside an invitation with a flippant retort — or relieved?

Zack was just a breath away from enfolding her in strong arms and catching her close, one vast ache of desire that went beyond the purely physical.

Alys had got under his skin, into the very heart of him, in a way that no other woman had managed, he admitted wryly. He was on the verge of loving her so much that it scared him. The sweet fire of her lips seared his very soul and threatened to leave him in a world of bleak longing for a girl who probably already belonged to another man.

Resisting the irresistible, he dropped his hands. . .

Alys felt bereft. Even without his arms about her, he had held her captive, surrounding her with a warmth and a wonderment that she didn't want to end.

She ached for more of him than one kiss with all its exciting, heart-stirring promise. But he moved away from her, completely in control in a way that shamed the wanton longing that besieged and almost betrayed her.

'You shouldn't have done that,' she said slowly, a little breathlessly, wondering if he knew the pound of her heart and the racing flame kindled by his kiss.

Zack smiled into hazel eyes filled with a misty delight that belied the soft reproach of the words. 'Shall I take it back?'

'No!' she exclaimed, hastily side-stepping in case he meant to carry out the laughing threat. 'I know I have to be on my guard with certain elements of the public but apparently SCOs can be just as much of a threat!' she added, putting a hand to her cap but finding that his kiss had been so light, so fleeting, that it was still securely in place. Obviously, she had only imagined that his lips had lingered for an eternity of delight.

'That's just the kind of false conclusion I expect from giggling junior nurses. I hoped you were learning to trust me,' he said in sudden impatience. 'I admit to playing the field in my youth and sowing a few wild oats, like almost every other overworked medical student, but those days are long behind me.'

His feelings soaring to the surface, Zack was about to assure her that she was the only girl he would ever want when Wanda swept into the room, stiff with suspicion.

Promptly, he reached for the X-ray folder and held it out to Alys. 'See to it that these follow Mrs Munro to the ward, please, Staff. . .' He said, briskly professional.

'Yes, Doctor.' Alys smiled innocently at the frowning casualty sister. 'Were you looking for me, Sister?'

'Wondering where you'd got to, certainly. Take those X-rays up to Gower Ward and then go to tea. I'll speak to you later. . .' Wanda looked her over with cold eyes, suspicious of the warm tinge of her cheeks and the sparkling eyes.

'Yes, Sister. . .' Glad to escape to cool her face and calm her racing heart, Alys turned away. As she closed the door behind her, she caught the first words of Wanda's crisp reproach.

'I hope you know what you're doing, Zack! That girl probably thinks you're really interested in her. . .'

Alys didn't wait to hear any more. . .

On her return to A and E, she was called into the office. Wanda indicated a chair with a pleasant smile. 'Sit down, Staff. I know you've been on your feet all day and what I want to say is off the record. I'm sure you won't mind a word of warning.'

The unexpected friendliness of her manner put Alys instantly on her guard. 'That sounds as if you think I've done something wrong.'

'Not *wrong* exactly. Irresponsible might be a better word,' Wanda amended.

'Is this something to do with Mr Burrows? If so, I'd like to put on record that he twisted our conversation out of all recognition!'

'This has nothing to do with a patient. I've no complaints about your work. It's your attitude that bothers me.'

Alys stiffened at that echo of Zack's words. 'I'm not sure what you mean, Sister.'

'I've been very patient all these weeks. But it's time I had a word with you about flirting with members of the staff. No, don't deny it,' she added lightly as Alys opened her mouth to protest. 'I don't want to know what was going on between you and the SCO but I'm sure you weren't studying X-ray plates!'

'No, Sister.' Alys smiled, heartened by the tolerant tone. Perhaps Wanda and Zack really were just friends and she wasn't annoyed because she'd caught them looking as if they'd just leaped out of each other's arms, she told herself — and hastily crushed the foolish flicker of hope.

Wanda's eyes narrowed at the unrepentant tone and self-satisfied smile, her jealous dislike of the staff nurse hardening. If Martin really wanted this girl, there was nothing to be done and she loved him enough to want his happiness. But she couldn't believe that Alys Mackenzie was right for him when the girl was so blatant in her encouragement of Zack!

'Perhaps you'd like to explain what you were doing in the emergency-room when there were patients waiting for attention?' she suggested coldly.

'I wanted a private word with Dr Howes. I'd just heard about his sister and——'

'You were on duty,' Wanda interrupted sharply. 'And you shouldn't be alone with any doctor in a room with the door shut unless you're discussing the care of a patient. But perhaps you don't care if people talk about you!'

Alys bridled. 'You know Dr Howes much better

than I do and you're frequently together in this room with the door shut! Isn't it *your* reputation that you should be worrying about, Sister?'

Wanda's mouth tightened. 'It's just because I know Dr Howes so much better that I'm giving you a friendly warning. And, while I'm on the subject, I suggest you tone down your relationship with Dr Kemp when you're on duty,' she added, although she had promised herself not to mention something so painful.

'I don't think you can accuse either of us of flaunting it,' Alys said in astonishment, puzzled by the acid resentment of the words. 'We're very discreet!'

Wanda's smile was sceptical. 'Yet everyone knows that you're romantically involved.'

'Nothing could stop the juniors from seeing romance around every corner. It brightens up the days for them. I don't mean to be rude, Sister,' she went on firmly, 'but my relationship with Dr Kemp or any other doctor is entirely my business and you really haven't any right to object as long as my work doesn't suffer.'

'I've a right to object when you're playing fast and loose with someone I care about, however!' Wanda retorted on a sudden storm of jealous rage.

'I'm a little confused,' Alys said slowly, bewildered by the casualty sister's fury. 'Are we talking about Dr Howes or Dr Kemp?'

Wanda smouldered. 'Does it matter? You're breaking the rules, in either case! You're employed to look after patients, not to spend your time trying to snare a husband!'

The rank injustice of the words fired Alys. 'Oh, I

see!' she said in deceptively dulcet tones. 'You're afraid that one of them might want to marry me!' She smoothed the folds of her uniform skirt carefully over her knees, the sparkle of anger in her hazel eyes. 'We both know that it isn't likely to be Zack so it must be Martin's interest in me that upsets you so much!'

'I've seen you hanging around him with smiles and soft words,' Wanda said bitterly, too angry for pride or caution. 'Running after Zack to make Martin want you all the more! And I'm not the only one to notice! You aren't pulling the wool over Zack's eyes, whatever you might think. He knows what you are — and I for one won't blame him if he takes advantage of it!'

'I think you've said enough, Sister — and I don't understand most of it!' Alys flared, leaping to her feet. 'But if I've got it right, you don't like me going out with Dr Kemp. But if that's the way *he* wants it, I don't see any reason why I should explain to you — or anyone else!'

Wanda's expression was glacial. 'How dare you use that tone to me, Nurse Mackenzie! Watch your step or you'll find yourself not just working in a different department but working at another hospital!' she warned icily, dark eyes flashing dislike. 'Go and get on with some work — but remember what I've said!'

'That you'll do your best to get me sacked if I talk to Zack or go out with Martin? Oh, I'll keep it in mind! If I can't resist flirting with every doctor in sight, at least I'll try not to do it under your nose!' A sharp slam of the door vented a little of Alys's temper, so seldom aroused, but there were tears of humiliation in her hazel eyes. How could Zack discuss her to her obvious detriment with someone who disliked her so much? It hurt that his interest in her was just as superficial as she had feared, too.

Observing her stormy face and suspiciously moist eyes, Nicola fell into step beside her with a smile of sympathy. 'In Sister's bad books again?'

'You won't believe what I've done this time!' Alys exclaimed bitterly. 'I've dared to date a man she wants — and we all thought that Zachary Howes was the love of her life!'

'Are you talking about Martin?' Nicola asked tentatively. 'They were very close at one time. I think she hoped to marry him but it suddenly went sour.'

'You're joking!' Alys exclaimed, startled.

'No, it's true enough. I thought you knew.'

'Martin's never said a word — and nor has anyone else! Not to me, anyway!' She wondered why no one had told her the reason for Wanda's marked dislike of her all these weeks.

'It was some time ago now and there's always something or somebody new for the juniors to talk about,' Nicola placated. 'It was yesterday's news by the time you arrived, I suppose.'

'But what went wrong?'

'I don't know who broke it off or why — but they just stopped seeing each other. They were still friends, though. It's only lately that they seem to be avoiding each other and I assumed that was because she's been dating Zack.' She added musingly, 'But if she's giving you stick because of Martin, she must still have a soft spot for him. . .'

Later, Alys was swabbing a teenager's badly gashed

leg when Zack arrived to examine the wound and she stepped back for him without even a smile, still angry that he had talked her over with Wanda.

'Very nasty,' he commented, exploring the extent of the deep cut on the sturdy thigh. 'How did it happen, Gary?'

The boy looked shifty. 'Climbed over a fence and caught it on a nail.'

'You'll need a tetanus jab if you haven't had one recently. You're a bit old for fence-climbing, aren't you?'

'Forgot my key. Mum was out but the back door's always unlocked.'

'Open invitation to burglars, eh?' Seeing the boy's face turn brick-red at his light words, he exchanged a glance with Alys. 'Fetch a suture kit, please, Staff. . .'

Alys was about to indicate the kidney dishes on the locker behind him, one with a prepared syringe of local anaesthetic and the other containing needle-holder and sutures, when she realised the meaningful message in his grey eyes and whisked from the cubicle, closing the curtains carefully behind her.

A burly policeman was in Reception, chatting up the prettier of the duty clerks, and he looked round at Alys. 'Has he confessed yet, Staff?' he asked with a cheerful grin. 'Little tearaway! I found him limping along an alley with blood pouring down his leg and all he says is that he was trying to get into his own back yard and fell off the fence.'

'And you don't believe him?'

'Let's just say that he had some unlikely articles in his pockets and looks like a lad who's breaking into houses while the owners are at work or out shopping. Looks innocent enough, doesn't he? Sings in the local church choir, too, he tells me.' He shook his head.

'What will happen to him?'

'I'm taking him down to the station as soon as he's had that leg seen to and I've managed to contact his mother. Try that number again, will you, love?' he added, turning back to the clerk.

Going back to the cubicle, Alys found the boy near to tears and Zack assuring him that he was unlikely to go to prison if it really was his first offence. 'It wouldn't be prison, anyway, at your age,' he added kindly. 'You'll probably get probation—but your mum won't be too pleased, will she?'

Gary shot a glance at Alys. 'I never took anything. I just liked to have a look round their houses,' he said defensively.

Alys was saddened by the admission. He looked such a nice lad. But appearances could be deceptive, she reminded herself. So could attitudes. Who would ever suspect from Zack's casual charm that his kiss could convey such breathtaking tenderness?

'It's still breaking and entering, Gary. And if the owners say that things are missing and you admit to being in their houses then it's hard for anyone to believe that you didn't take them, isn't it?' Zack pointed out reasonably.

'You don't believe me, either,' the boy said sullenly.

'I'm not judge or jury. You don't have to convince me. Or explain anything to me. Save it for your mum.' Zack injected the local anaesthetic and then drew Alys from the cubicle. 'Little idiot,' he said tolerantly, out of the boy's hearing. 'Got into bad company at school and says all his mates are playing truant and breaking into likely-looking houses. He's more clever than most, though. He chose a neighbour's house and almost convinced the constable who found him that he'd been trying to get into his own garden, two doors down. Claimed the fences were lower.'

'He doesn't look like a burglar.'

He smiled down at her. 'That angelic face probably deceives his neighbours, too.'

'What is he? Thirteen, fourteen?'

'Older than he looks, Alys. Nearly sixteen. Old enough to want to impress girlfriends by spending money on them that he can't get by honest means.'

'But he said he hadn't actually stolen anything!'

'He admitted it to me. He just didn't want you to know that he's a thief.' Zack paused to look down at her with a twinkle in his grey eyes. 'He's old enough to notice a pretty nurse when he sees one, too. He says you're a lovely girl — and he's right. You *are*.'

Flustered by the low words and the warmth of his smile, Alys knew she was blushing to the roots of her hair as Wanda looked towards them with suspicion-narrowed eyes.

Working in A and E would no longer be such a delight to her if she had to contend with open hostility from the casualty sister as well as open admiration from the SCO, she thought wryly. . .

CHAPTER SEVEN

MARTIN headed towards them and the moment of affinity between herself and Zack was lost. 'You're going to Link Lodge after work, aren't you, Alys? It's a beast of a journey by bus. I'm off duty at five and I'll take you,' he told her in a proprietorial tone.

'It's very nice of you but there's really no need,' Alys assured him hastily. 'It's right out of your way. . .'

It was some time since she had managed to fit in a visit to her mother and she was looking forward to doing so that evening. The former Sister Wells, still remembered by colleagues and some patients at St Benet's, had decided against returning to hospital nursing and was now the matron of Link Lodge, a council-funded nursing home in Amble.

'Link Lodge?' Zack echoed swiftly. 'My old nanny is a resident and it's about time I paid her a visit. It isn't out of *my* way and you're very welcome to a lift, Alys.'

She wished Martin anywhere but hovering impatiently at her elbow. 'I'm spoiled for choice!' she laughed, knowing she really had no choice at all when Martin's scowl dared her to accept and a grim-faced casualty sister was looking and listening and waiting to pounce. 'But I think I'd better take the bus. . .'

With his long stride, Zack followed in her wake as

she went off duty and caught up with her as she paused on the steps outside the hospital, appreciating the fresh air and the early evening sunshine after a long day in A and E.

As she turned, sensing his approach, he smiled at the slender girl whose fragile prettiness caught so fiercely at his heart. 'My offer of a lift still stands.'

Alys looked up at him, terribly tempted by the charm of his smile and warmed by his unmistakable interest.

'Ready, Alys? Shall we make a move before the rush-hour traffic builds up?' Martin appeared at her side, forestalling acceptance.

Claiming her, she thought crossly—but it was her own fault for becoming more involved with him than she had ever intended. . .or wanted.

'Oh, Martin! I thought you'd gone. . .' He had left A and E some time before without making a definite arrangement to meet her when she went off duty, much to her relief.

'I said I'd take you to Amble.' Martin scowled at Zack who smiled back blandly, infuriatingly aware of his irritation and inviting another punch on the nose in spite of his powerful build and newly discovered boxing skills. Martin wished that Alys wouldn't encourage the man with her pretty smile. Why the devil couldn't he be content with Wanda and leave the susceptible staff nurse to him?

'Well, if you're sure. . .' Alys did her best to hide her reluctance, longing for an excuse to avoid arriving at Link Lodge with Martin in tow.

Her mother would leap to all the wrong conclusions—and he didn't need any encouragement to make more of their friendship! He was already hinting at a long-term relationship and obliquely suggesting that she should move in with him. Alys wondered how he had become so sure of her in such a short time when she had tried so hard to keep him at arm's length. His breezy confidence was the least attractive facet of his character when compared with Zack's unassuming charm. . .

She was swept towards his car with Zack's amused eyes boring into her back. Before she slid into the passenger seat, she glanced back to see Zack greet the emerging casualty sister with a smile that confirmed their closeness, and her heart faltered.

Martin had seen, too. 'Seems to be serious, doesn't it?' he said airily. He couldn't object, in the circumstances, but he didn't approve. 'They've been going out for some weeks and it's my guess he'd marry her tomorrow if only she'd say yes,' he added with the deliberate intent of steering her romantic tendencies away from Zachary Howes and towards himself.

It was common gossip—and hadn't Zack confirmed it days ago? So Alys didn't understand the pain and the panic that clutched at her breast. There was nothing between herself and Zack but a few foolish words and an even more foolish kiss!

'She's very attractive,' she said stiffly, surprised that Martin seemed so unaffected by his former girlfriend's deepening involvement with another man. Perhaps the loving had all been on Wanda's side and he truly didn't care if it had been transferred to Zack.

Martin nodded. 'Clever, too. If she'd shown the

slightest sign of wanting to marry him, he'd have ditched her by now,' he said cynically, determined to paint his colleague as black as possible.

Alys wondered if he was as indifferent as he pretended and what had gone wrong between the CO and the casualty sister. Unless she'd misunderstood, Wanda was still in love with Martin. Perhaps his fierce dislike of Zack was due to jealousy and a lingering affection for Wanda. As for Zack, he wanted to marry Wanda—hadn't he admitted as much? But he had kissed *her* with a tenderness that implied much more than a fleeting sexual stir, she recalled wistfully.

It was all very puzzling. . .

Just as she'd expected, her mother's face visibly brightened when she arrived with Martin. It seemed to worry her that Alys took so little interest in men and marriage although she had been warning her daughter since her earliest training days against romantic involvement with doctors!

'It's lovely to see you, darling,' Marian Mackenzie said warmly, her curious gaze riveted on the tall young man with his blond hair and fresh face and pleasant smile. 'It's been some time since you've been to visit me. . .'

'Things have been a bit hectic lately. . .oh, this is Dr Kemp—Martin! One of our COs.' She had mentioned him once or twice, probably giving her matchmaking mother cause to hope, but now she did her best to imply with her deliberately offhand attitude and casual tone that her relationship with Martin was purely professional. Seeing the smile that welcomed him, she doubted if her mother was deceived.

A smiling Martin shook hands with the tall, slim woman who was unmistakably a mature edition of Alys. 'I'm delighted to meet you at last, Mrs Mackenzie. . .or should I say Sister Wells? You're a Benny's legend, you know!' he said warmly.

The reminder pleased her, just as he had intended. 'The good old days,' she said wistfully. 'They seem a very long time ago now, I'm afraid. But Benny's doesn't change very much, I'm glad to say. You'll stay and have some supper with us, I hope?'

It was exactly the outcome that Alys had feared, but there was nothing she could do about it. Her mother obviously approved of Martin and was no doubt already deciding on her wedding outfit! He was the kind of man that any mother would probably welcome as a son-in-law — charming, clever, confident — and a doctor to boot!

But Alys instinctively balked at the thought of marrying Martin and had a sudden vision of herself in bridal white walking down the aisle towards a tall, powerfully built and very attractive man who beamed his lasting love for her with a slow, heart-stopping smile in speaking grey eyes.

It was an unlikely dream and she crushed the fleeting suspicion that loving Zachary Howes might be her destiny. One kiss couldn't sweep a girl into lasting and unchanging love all in a moment. . .not when she took such care to protect her vulnerable heart from such a folly.

'He's charming,' Marian whispered a little later as Alys helped to bring the plates to the table. 'I *do* like him, darling.' She beamed approval at the daughter who seemed so stubbornly resistant to romance. 'I really can't remember the last time you brought a young man to meet me.'

'I didn't bring Martin to meet you,' Alys said sternly. 'He offered me a lift and it seemed silly to refuse when the buses are so unreliable.'

Her mother's smile was knowing. 'If you say so, Alys. But I think there's more to it than just driving you twenty miles to see your mother. Isn't he the same man who took you to the midsummer ball last week?'

Alys sighed. 'You're as bad as the first-years,' she chided, exasperated by her mother's romantic tendency to make far too much of a very ordinary date. 'Going to the midsummer ball with someone doesn't mean that I'm about to marry him! Martin's just a friend!'

Her mother studied her soberly. 'Darling, I know your father and I made a mess of things but we were never really suited. You're much too sensible to make that mistake.'

Alys smiled, a little wryly. 'When love walks in the door, sense flies out of the window!'

Marian sighed. 'You're too young to be so cynical, Alys. . .and you shouldn't be so afraid of loving, even if it doesn't always bring the happiness people hope it will.'

'"Better to have loved and lost"?' she suggested lightly, knowing that she *was* afraid to give her heart, particularly to a man who might not want it.

'Yes,' Marian said surprisingly. 'Loving, even in vain, gives a greater insight into the feelings of others. You may suffer dreadful heartache rather than the happiness you hope and you'll certainly be quite convinced that you'll never love so much again. But it's all part of life's rich tapestry even if you can't make out the pattern at the time.'

'I suppose I am rather wary where men are concerned,' Alys admitted, realising that her mother was feeling guilty in case she had allowed her own disappointment and bitterness to colour her daughter's attitudes. 'Daddy let us both down so badly. . .'

'It needn't happen to you. And if it should—well, without the shadows how can you appreciate the sunshine, Alys, dear?' Marian said gently. 'Nursing is a wonderful career but I'd like to see you happily married and I'm sure *you* won't make the mistake of falling in love with a totally unsuitable man, as I did. You've a very level head on your shoulders.'

Alys smiled but she was troubled by a suspicion that it might already be too late to avoid the mistake of falling in love with Zachary Howes—and what could be more unsuitable than that?

Before she and Martin left, Marian showed them round Link Lodge with its well-planned amenities for the elderly residents. The place had a happy feel about it and it was obvious that Sister Wells had found her niche once more. Alys knew how much her mother had missed her ward at Benny's and how many unhappy years she had endured with her father.

They had been so obviously mismatched that it was a puzzle to Alys why they had ever married. Love could blind, and confuse and hurtle people into relationships that had small chance of survival. Was it so surprising that she had always backed away from the merest hint of it? But perhaps her mother was right and she should allow herself to love without reservation, whatever the outcome — and maybe she would be fortunate enough to know the sunshine without the shadows. . .

'I liked your mother,' Martin said on the way home. 'She's charming. . .warm and friendly. Just like her daughter.' He smiled at her.

'She liked you, too,' Alys said stiffly, feeling that her mother's apparent approval had probably set the seal on their relationship as far as Martin was concerned and rather annoyed about it. They *weren't* a couple, no matter how it seemed to the world.

He was pleased but unsurprised. 'It would be nice for you to meet my parents, don't you think? Why not come to Hampshire with me on my next trip home at the end of the month?' That should convince Wanda that he no longer cared *and* stop Zack in his tracks!

'We'll see,' Alys compromised, but she had no intention of meeting his family on the understanding that their relationship might lead to marriage!

'If he's getting too serious then tell him so!' Wynne urged when Alys confided in her that night.

She tightened the belt of her silk robe about her slender waist, fresh from the shower, blonde hair damp-darkened and framing her pretty face with tight curls. 'I've tried! He doesn't listen when I say I just want to be friends — and now he's met my mother he probably imagines that the future is all cut and dried! Her own marriage was a disaster but she can't wait to see me settled with a husband!'

'Mothers are like that,' Wynne sympathised. 'They can't relax until we're safely married.'

'Well, I'm not marrying Martin just to please mine!' Her mouth set in an obstinate line.

'Has he asked you?' Wynne asked curiously as she sweetened a mug of steaming cocoa for her friend.

'No — and I hope he never does! I like him a lot but that isn't enough, is it?' She couldn't admit, even to her very understanding friend, that Martin's kisses left her completely cold or that she found herself fantasising about Zachary Howes in his arms.

'So what will you do? Stop seeing him?'

'I really don't know what to do. He can be very good company — when he isn't hinting that he's my destiny.' Alys sighed. 'But it isn't worth the conflict with Wanda Nelson. If it isn't Martin, it's Zachary Howes — I just wish she'd make up her mind which of them she wants!' she said bitterly.

Wynne curled up on the sofa, settling down for a cosy gossip. 'Martin dropped her like a hot brick once he knew she was hearing wedding bells.'

Alys shot her a reproachful glance. 'It seems that everyone but me knew they had something going at one time! You might have warned me, Wynne! You know Wanda has been gunning for me ever since my first day in A and E.'

'I thought she was over him. After all, she made a beeline for Zack when he came back as SCO and they've dated regularly ever since.'

'As if that means anything!' Alys knew from her own experience that dating one man didn't stop a girl from hankering after another.

'It could mean that she's given up hoping to marry Martin,' Wynne said sagely. 'She isn't the type to let another woman have a man she still wants.'

'There isn't much she can do about it if he doesn't want her, is there? Except make life difficult for me.'

Her friend looked sceptical. 'If some girl was dating a man you wanted, wouldn't you make a push to get him? Move heaven and earth, if necessary? If she *does* want Martin then be prepared to lose him sooner or later — and be really sure that *you* don't want him!'

Wynne made it sound easy, Alys thought with a sigh as she rinsed the empty mugs. As if just wanting a man was the surefire route to getting him!

She wanted Zack, she finally admitted as she climbed between cool sheets and snuggled into soft pillows, wishing his strong arms were reaching to enfold her. But she believed that she was sufficiently in control to keep her emotions — and Zack — firmly at bay. . .

The victims of a gas explosion in a local factory were shared between St Benet's and another local hospital and all her time and energies were taken up with the work she had been trained to do. Alys had very few moments to think about Zack or the vivid dreams of him that had given her a restless night, as shrill ambulance sirens announced the arrival of each casualty, newly dug from the debris.

Many of them were girls about her own age. The blast had stripped skin from young faces and hair from once-pretty heads and flying glass had done further damage. The resulting fire had caused serious burns in some cases. Every available nurse was called from the wards and off-duty staff came in to help as soon as news of the disaster spread.

Alys forgot the rankling resentment of the casualty sister's accusations as she worked beside her, setting up drips and blood transfusions, preparing patients for emergency surgery, suturing and dressing minor wounds. The two girls cut away remnants of clothing, washed away blood and dust and debris, soothed fears and dried tears and dealt with the dazed and bewildered victims while in the emergency-room and casualty area and even out in the corridors over-stretched doctors and surgeons tended the more seriously injured.

'I can't see!' screamed one young girl, clawing desperately at Alys with ribboned hands that had taken the worst of the blast. 'I can't see. . .!'

Alys placed a strip of gauze across the eyes with their singed lashes, hoping that it was only a temporary blindness. 'Shock can play some strange tricks,' she soothed. 'Try not to worry, Wendy. Doctor will be here soon to look at your eyes. . .'

She had just finished putting a temporary dressing on hands that awaited the attention of a plastic surgeon when Roy Henry, the opthalmic surgeon, drew back the cubicle curtains. Wendy's bandaged hands clung tightly to hers in spite of their agony as she endured the brief examination that preceded the expected verdict of immediate surgery.

Wondering if even the clever surgeon's skill could restore badly damaged optic nerves, Alys did everything she could to cheer and reassure the badly fright-

ened girl until her shocked husband arrived to support
her.

Then, hearing Zack's urgent shout from a neigh-
bouring cubicle, she sped to his side. His patient had
arrived in deep shock but with no obvious injuries.
Detecting a dangerously slow heartbeat and labouring
lungs, he had diagnosed heart failure, supplied oxygen
and medication and wired her up to a monitor.

Without warning, the girl's heart had stopped and
he had instantly swung into the procedure for rescuscitation, knowing the crash team were fighting for yet
another young life in the emergency-room.

'Take over!' he commanded, seeing a Benny's uniform and a pair of trained hands rather than Alys as
she came to assist. Easing her hands into position
beneath his, she continued with the steady, rhythmic
pumping as he straightened. 'I'll be right back. . .' he
promised and disappeared with a flurry of curtains.

With every push, Alys forced air into the collapsed
lungs and oxygen into the bloodstream until Zack
returned with a filled hypodermic and plunged the
needle directly into the ventricle of the girl's heart.

Gazes on the silent monitor, they waited for the
drug to take effect and then exchanged satisfied
glances as leads picked up and conveyed the renewed
heartbeat to the screen and the signal promptly echoed
it's reassuring rhythm.

'The prognosis isn't good, I'm afraid,' Zack sighed
as the patient was whisked away to the intensive-care
unit. 'But we may have given her a fighting chance
between us.' His eyes were friendly as he smiled at the
weary staff nurse in her soiled and bloodied apron,

cap knocked askew as she worked on the patient, and
thought how dearly he loved her even if this wasn't the
moment to think it or declare it.

Warmed by the words that linked their recent efforts
and probably gave her more credit than she deserved,
Alys smiled back, his niceness melting a little more of
the ice that had protected her heart from the perils of
loving for the last four years. . .

CHAPTER EIGHT

SHE wasn't a party person, Alys admitted, crushed between Martin and one of his cronies, nursing a glass of cheap plonk and trying to take an intelligent interest in the finer points of rugger as the two men enlarged on the afternoon's game.

Her idea of an evening out was a show followed by supper in an intimate restaurant with someone who didn't talk sport or cars, she decided wistfully as a couple barged into her on their way across the crowded room. It was only a small flat and it seemed that half of Benny's had turned up to help the owner celebrate his surgical fellowship.

Her bored gaze swept the room and found Zack and her heart gave a start of surprised delight — until she saw that he was with Wanda and then it plummeted.

'All right, darling?' Martin paused in his recounting of the great try he'd scored to send her an absent smile and utter the equally absent words.

'It's so hot in here. I'm going to find a breath of air.' Alys wriggled from under his arm and pushed through the press of people, mostly strangers, wondering if Martin would mind — or notice — if she simply went home.

Managing to mislay her unwanted wine, she reached the French doors that opened on to the unkempt garden of the basement flat. It was a lovely evening,

too good to waste on a party and people with whom
she had little in common but Benny's.

'Shall we run away together?'

Her face lit up in response to the deep, humorous
voice in her ear and she turned with a sudden smile for
Zack, standing beside her with a bottle of champagne
and two glasses. 'Hello. I didn't expect to see you here.'

'Wanda dragged me along.'

'Oh. . .yes, of course.' She glanced towards the
casualty sister, looking beautiful in ice-blue silk that
complemented her dark hair and warm skin. 'She
seems to be enjoying it all.'

'She loves a party.'

'So do I when I know most of the other guests,' Alys
defended as if his words had implied that she was a
party pooper. 'These are mostly Martin's friends.'

Zack's warm grey eyes were understanding as he
smiled down at her. 'Shall we run away together?' he
repeated, admiring her slight figure in the multi-
coloured skirt and peach silk top, her high heels
bringing her riot of fair curls just level with his
shoulder.

Her smile was almost wistful. 'Don't tempt me!'

'No one would miss us.'

She looked across the room at Martin, glass in hand,
fair face flushed as he vied with his friend in the
recounting of past successes on the rugger field, and
then at Wanda, flirting outrageously with an unknown
man. 'Not at the moment, anyway,' she conceded.

Zack tucked the champagne under his arm and took
her hand firmly in his own. 'We can explore the
rainforest, at least. . .'

Alys let him draw her into the overgrown garden although her fast-beating heart was drumming a warning. The warm clasp of his hand sent a thrill of anticipation rippling along every vein.

They weren't the only guests to escape from the heat and the crush. People sat or sprawled on the scrubby lawn, wandered up and down weed-ridden paths, sheltered under the heavy summer foliage of tall trees.

'I didn't know Guy was such a popular chap,' Zack remarked as they picked their way through a number of recumbent bodies, avoiding glasses and paper plates of half-eaten food, heading for the distant end of the long garden.

'He probably doesn't know most of them,' Alys pointed out from her experience of such parties. 'Me, for one. . .'

'You came with Kemp, I suppose?'

'Yes.' And you brought Wanda, she added silently. But they had abandoned their partners to steal away, hand in hand, like a couple of naughty children, she thought happily, as he popped the champagne like an expert. Alys smiled at him over its sparkle. 'Now this is what I call a party!' she declared with a glimmer of laughter in her hazel eyes.

'Two's company. . .' Zack agreed softly.

She was so pretty with the fair curls framing her heart-shaped face and teasing her slender neck, the candid eyes with their silky sweep of long lashes and the tremulous mouth that invited kissing. But it wasn't just her prettiness in the colourful skirt, emphasising her tiny waist, and the silk vest hinting at small sweet breasts that caught at his heart.

He bent his head to kiss her, tasting the linger of champagne on her lips and testing her response. Alys leaned against him, revelling in the warmth of his mouth and sensing the heat of desire in his powerful body.

It couldn't be that a mere mouthful of champagne had gone to her head. She couldn't blame the moonlight for the sun hadn't yet set on that midsummer evening. But she was in the thrall of an enchantment that urged her to put an arm about his neck and draw his head down for another of the kisses that sent liquid fire rampaging through her veins.

Zack took her glass from nerveless fingers, set it with his own and the champagne on the ground, and drew her into his arms. Alys sighed contentedly as she was clasped at last to that powerful chest, so close that she could feel the thud of his heart against her breast. As he smiled down at her, she looked back at him through a mist of desire that she made no effort to conceal.

'I've wanted to hold you like this for so long,' he said with an ache of longing, stroking the soft hair from her face.

Alys held her breath in anticipation as his long, clever fingers slowly traced a path from the glow of her cheek to the silk of her throat and lower to the shadowed hollow. A shudder of delight ran through her as his hand closed over a soft curve and a thumb swept tantalisingly over the hardening bud of her breast.

His mouth sought hers, hard and seeking, urgent with desire, and the fire of his longing ignited her own.

She wound her arms about him, giving kiss for kiss, body urging ever-closer to the hard leanness of his tall frame.

Then, suddenly, she was afraid of the soaring passion she aroused in him with her yielding promise of surrender. He wasn't a man to listen to no if she had seemed to be saying yes all evening with her smiles and too eager response. Hadn't she always vowed to love the man who eventually swept her over the threshold between virginity and fulfilled womanhood? And she wasn't in love with Zack, was she?

She captured the hand that was playing such havoc with her senses as he stroked and caressed the warm mound of her breast. She eased her mouth away from the kisses that tempted her beyond all resistance and reluctantly drew herself from his exciting embrace.

'No. . .' she said firmly as Zack looked his disappointment and tried to draw her back into his arms. 'I mean it, Zack!' She evaded him with a militancy in her hazel eyes that gave him pause. 'I know this kind of thing goes on at parties but it isn't my style.'

'Nor mine,' he told her swiftly, wounded by her dismissal of those magic moments as a party exercise born of alcohol and propinquity. Perhaps the ardent encounter meant little to Alys but Zack knew he would never, ever forget the wonder of holding her close or the impact on his heart and his hopes for the future of her sweet, yielding kisses.

'That isn't the way I hear it.' Alys didn't dare to believe what she saw in his eyes for that way led to possible heartache and humiliation. The talk of him as a Lothario, true or not, was always in her mind, keeping her from trusting him with her heart and her happiness.

'You're talking to the wrong people. Kemp has an axe to grind — and the juniors are just echoing long-ago legends.' His tone was impatient.

'No smoke without fire,' she challenged, thinking of the blaze that seemed to exist between SCO and Casualty Sister.

'That's exactly the attitude that drove me from Hartlake and a consultancy that was just within my grasp!' he said angrily.

'I thought you left because of some trouble over a woman.'

His eyes narrowed. 'You could say that but I've heard it phrased better. I thought Kemp would see that as a golden opportunity to blacken my name. He's held a grudge ever since I beat him to a junior registrar's post years ago!'

Alys felt her heart sink. Martin hadn't enlarged but he had hinted at an indiscreet affair, perhaps with a patient, and Zack didn't appear to be denying it — her instinctive resistance to losing her heart and perhaps her virginity to a man too like her father for comfort hardened all over again.

'Speaking of Martin, he must be wondering what's happened to me,' she said brightly. 'I ought to go and find him. I did come to this party with him, after all. . .'

'And you'll be leaving with him, I suppose.'

Zack's mouth set in an uncompromising line. There had been so much golden promise in her smiling eyes and warm lips but her readiness to think ill of him and her desire to rush back to Kemp led him to believe he'd misread the signs. She didn't seem the kind to flirt, to lead a man on and then disappoint him, but what else was he to think?

'Yes, of course. . .'

He would be taking Wanda home when the party was over! How could he possibly object if she left with Martin? A few kisses didn't give him the right to vet her friends or to censure her actions! Certainly not while he was apparently spending his leisure hours with the casualty sister. . .

Wanda was in an exceptionally good mood when Alys arrived for work the next morning. 'Great party last night, wasn't it?' she said in friendly greeting.

'Marvellous,' Alys agreed dutifully.

She had persuaded Martin to take her home at an early hour and could only imagine how late it had been when the party finally broke up—and how it had ended for Wanda, judging by the shine of triumph in her eyes and her Cheshire-cat smile.

She indicated the benches filling with patients. 'Looks like being another busy day,' she said hastily, hoping to deter Wanda from detailing all the delights of the previous night.

'So it does. You can start by seeing to the biker in Cubicle Six.' Wanda smothered a huge yawn and laughed. 'Oh, dear! Shows I haven't had much sleep, doesn't it?'

A perfectly innocent remark. Or was it? Alys wondered, suspecting an almost feline satisfaction behind the smiling words. Turning away, she was surprised by the wrench of pain in her breast. She had suspected for weeks that Zack and Wanda were lovers so why should the reminder hurt so much?

She concentrated on swabbing mud and blood from the torn face of a motorcyclist who had taken a corner too fast and overturned. For all her care, he yelled a pained protest.

Following the sound, Zack saw from her face that hurting anyone, even if necessary or unavoidable, came hard to her. Sometimes he felt she was too sensitive, but she was just the thoughtful, caring kind of nurse they needed in the profession.

She moved the bowl with its bloody swabs and made way for him to examine the patient. 'Let's have a look at that face of yours, old chap. . .' His expert fingers explored the damage. 'I suspect you've cracked a cheekbone as well as your nose and I'm not too happy about the look of your jaw, either. I'll order some X-rays and I'll get one of our orthopaedic wizards to have a look at you. In the meantime, I'm afraid there's still some cleaning up to be done.' The man muttered something that sounded like an expletive and shot a wary glance at Alys. 'Be gentle with him, Nurse,' Zack added with a twinkle in his grey eyes.

Her answering smile was cool, discouraging him from supposing that she recalled those party kisses with any pleasure, and as she continued to bathe the deep cuts Zack felt the distinct chill of her attitude. He wondered if he had committed some sin without knowing it. Women were the very devil at times — and this one seemed to be firmly in his blood for all his efforts to ignore her insidious appeal.

Wanda's dark head appeared between the folds of

the chintz curtains. 'We need you, Zack — motorway pile-up! The first casualties are just coming in. . .'

'Right. . . I'll be with you in two ticks!' He turned to Alys as the casualty sister sped away. 'Get a junior to take over from you here, Staff. It sounds as though we'll need as many experienced nurses as we can get. . .'

The piercing wail of an arriving ambulance coincided with his urgent departure for the emergency-room. Handing over to a first-year, Alys hurried after him, arriving as the first of a new batch of victims of motorway madness were rushed in by the paramedics.

Throughout a long morning, ambulances continued to bring in the badly injured and burned and surgeons were summoned from ward or clinic or lecture-room to make expert assessments and perform emergency surgery. Alys set up drips and prepared injections as the doctors battled to open an airway or stem bleeding, performing minor miracles even as they diagnosed the extent of injuries.

It had been a particularly bad incident, a lorry skidding out of control and slamming into an oncoming car and drivers of other fast-moving vehicles unable to avoid the knock-on effect. Police and fire-brigade vehicles and ambulances had arrived on the scene within minutes but couldn't save some lives or do much about the awful carnage of crushed and burning cars.

A total of twenty-four people were brought to Benny's during the day, some of them cut out of the wreckage and some only slightly injured or severely shocked. Along with everyone else, Alys skipped meal

breaks and stayed on duty well into the evening to do
what she could wherever she could as all non-urgent
admissions and operations were cancelled and extra
staff was called in for post-operative or intensive-care
nursing.

In the thick of it all, she found herself dealing with
a drunken hooligan who'd punched his hand through a
plate-glass window. He was foul-mouthed and cock-
sure and bled all over her apron as she stitched the
deep cuts and applied dressings.

A nurse was expected to keep cool in any situation
and it took only the wrong word or look for a difficult
patient to turn nasty, she knew from past experience.
Physical assault wasn't unknown in A and E but so far
Alys had escaped by jollying along likely assailants
with cheerful words and a smile that was careful not to
condemn but could unfortunately give the wrong
impression at times.

Alys didn't find it easy to conceal her feelings as she
tended a self-inflicted injury while men and women
who had been peacefully driving to work or going on
holiday or visiting families had suddenly been swept
into a carnage that had cost some their lives and others
their limbs.

'Don't need one of those, darling,' she was blithely
told when she suggested a tetanus injection, usual in
such cases. 'I'm a good healer. Good in other ways,
too.'

As the young lout leered at her, she continued to
unroll the gauze bandage neatly about his damaged
hand as if she was both blind and deaf to innuendo.

Suddenly his arm shot about her waist and he

grabbed at her breast. 'Want to try me out? I come highly recommended! Ask any of my tarts. Meet me tonight in the Greyhound and I'll give you the best night of your life,' he promised confidently. 'And that uniform is a great turn-on so don't forget to wear it!'

'Thanks but no, thanks,' Alys said firmly, moving from his unwelcome grasp with a hint of distaste in her expressive face.

Taking instant umbrage, he snarled at her angrily. 'Not bleeding good enough for you, is that it? Prefer one of these smart-ass doctors, do you? I bet you get up to a few naughties behind these curtains whenever the bloody sister isn't looking!'

This time, Martin wasn't around to come to her aid, being off duty and missing all the action, but the curtain was abruptly whisked back to admit a smouldering Zack who was struggling with a strong desire to put the uncouth young hooligan firmly in his place.

'This is the young man who put his hand through a window, is it? All taken care of, Staff?'

'Except for the tetanus jab, Doctor.'

'Told her I don't want one of them bleeding things, Doc.'

'Then I gather that you've had one recently, Mr Arnold?

'Nah. . .never had one. Don't believe in 'em.'

'That's a pity. It's a particularly nasty way to go and I really don't think you should take the risk. More people die from tetanus than you obviously realise — everything ready, Staff?'

With a reassuring smile for Alys, he took the syringe

from the kidney dish, thrust up the man's sleeve and gripped his arm with unmistakable intent.

He shrank back in obvious dread. 'No! Don't do that, Doc—please, mate! I don't like needles and I don't need a jab! Leave it out, will ya?' he protested urgently, endeavouring to release himself from that determined and very strong grasp of his arm.

'Would you hold his other arm for me, Staff? Don't struggle, Mr Arnold—or the needle will break and I shall have to do it all over again.'

Ignoring both curses and pleas, Zack slid in the hypodermic needle and released the plunger. After the injection, the patient sat with his head in his hands, complaining that he felt faint and wanted to be sick, acting more like ten than twenty-five so that Alys wondered why she had felt so threatened by him.

'Thanks,' she murmured gratefully, following Zack from the cubicle.

'I thought he was an ugly customer when I saw him on arrival. Giving you a hard time, wasn't he?'

He didn't tell her that he'd overheard some of the man's remarks but they had made his blood boil and it had taken all his time to remember that he was a physician with a duty to patients that didn't include taking them apart when they insulted one of the nurses.

Even when that nurse was coming to mean too much for comfort. . .

CHAPTER NINE

At the end of the day, Alys was exhausted, both emotionally and physically. Apart from tending the badly injured, a great many demands had been made on her by distressed relatives and shocked patients with only minor injuries that still needed expert medical care from weary nursing staff.

She collapsed into a chair in the empty office and kicked off her flat-heeled brogues and relaxed for a few moments, too tired even to think about going home. Thoughts drifting over the day, she didn't hear Zack's silent entry and he stood looking down at her tenderly.

Suddenly sensing his scrutiny, Alys sat up straight and opened her eyes, heart lurching as she met his smiling gaze.

'Are you all right?' he asked gently.

She nodded. 'Tired, that's all. Giving my poor feet a break before I make tracks for home.' She wriggled cramped toes as she spoke and Zack instantly crouched to take a slender, black-stockinged foot into both hands to massage the ache from sole and instep with strong but gentle strokes. It seemed such a natural gesture of concern from a naturally kind and caring man that Alys was undisturbed by the intimacy in spite of its undeniably erotic overtones. 'The healing touch,'

she told him with a grateful smile as he transferred his
attention to the other foot.

'Feel better?'

'Much!' It seemed just as natural to put a hand on
his broad shoulder and lean forward to kiss his cheek
and he smiled at her, releasing her foot with a last,
affectionate pat. Then he straightened and went away,
just in time to save her from a scold as Wanda arrived
for the evening handover to the relieving team of
nurses.

After the golden evening of Guy's party, it had been
another cold, wet day that made a mockery of summer
and Alys shivered slightly as she waited for her bus in
the grey drizzle, raincoat over her uniform dress.
Huddled in the sanctuary of the bus shelter, a little
saddened as she recalled the sights and sounds of the
day, she didn't notice the sleekly expensive car that
slowed to a halt beside her until the driver leaned to
open the passenger door.

'I'm going your way, Alys. . .jump in!' She obeyed
almost without thinking and the car shot away as soon
as she was settled. Zack sent her a twinkling, gently
amused glance. 'You looked like an orphan of the
storm.'

She stiffened, feeling that he constantly caught her
at a disadvantage. 'You needn't have stopped. A bus
would have been along shortly. It's a very good
service.'

It was ungracious but she couldn't help feeling that
she put more than her heart in jeopardy by seeing so
much of a man who constantly undermined her resolve
to keep him at a distance.

Zack understood both her weariness and her wariness but the fierce longing for her drove him on. 'Little miss independent,' he murmured. 'The pleasure is all mine, believe me. We don't see enough of each other.'

Her glance was sceptical. 'We spend hours of every day in each other's company.'

'That isn't what I meant and you know it. Why don't we stop off for a drink somewhere? You look as if you need to unwind.'

The warm concern in his deep voice and the niceness of his smile brought a rush of threatening tears, her emotions much too near the surface.

She sent him a shaky smile in return. 'I'm shattered, actually,' she admitted on a sudden rush. 'It's been quite a day.'

Zack removed a hand from the steering-wheel to brush a hovering tear from her cheek. His touch was very light, incredibly tender. 'It's good that you can still cry after all these years as a nurse,' he approved warmly, knowing the heart she always brought to her care of patients with a variety of problems.

She looked ruefully unsure. 'I'm always being told to toughen up. A good nurse shouldn't get emotionally involved with patients—or so we were taught during training.'

'The best nurses are always involved and never stop caring, Alys. It doesn't mean that you can't keep a cool head in a crisis or know just how to make someone feel better about things. For instance, you said all the right things to that poor woman who lost both her husband and daughter today.'

Alys sighed. 'Do you think so? What *is* the right thing when such things happen?'

'It's hard to know,' he agreed soberly. He turned to her with a smile in his grey eyes that lightened the mood. 'Anyway, after such an upsetting day, I thought you'd appreciate a lift home. It's a nasty night.'

'I do. It was a nice thought, Zack.' The warm response atoned for her earlier sharpness.

Briefly, he rested his hand on the taut fingers wrapped together in her lap. 'It's easy to be nice to you, sweetheart.'

She laughed. 'Flatterer!'

But the soft-spoken endearment and the tenderness in his touch had taken her by surprise and she hastily looked away from the warmly smiling eyes that invited her into the dangerous waters of mutual attraction.

A wry smile glinted in the grey eyes. 'Why do you never believe anything I say, Alys?'

'Because I suspect too many girls have, to their cost,' she retorted, his words shattering the breathless moment.

He sighed. 'What do I have to do to convince you that you've nothing to fear from the way I feel about you?'

She wasn't about to admit that she was much more frightened of her own feelings. 'You could try keeping your distance,' she suggested levelly.

'I will—if that's really what you want.' Waiting for traffic-lights to change from red to green, he bent his dark head to look into her serious face. 'Is it?'

Alys nodded. 'Yes.' Her tone defied the instinctive protest of her heart.

'Sure? So you won't let me buy you dinner?'

'Tonight. . .?' Alys was weakening before the quiet charm of his smile.

'We've earned it, haven't we?' he coaxed.

There were a number of very good reasons why it would be most unwise to spend the rest of the evening in his company but Alys heard herself agreeing on a surge of gratified delight.

Drawing up outside the tall block of flats, Zack leaned to brush her lips with just the hint of a kiss. 'I'll come back for you in an hour. . .'

She watched the car recede into the distance, knowing Martin would act hurt and disapproving when he found out about her date with the SCO and knowing that, madness or not, nothing would keep her from being ready and waiting when Zack came back for her. . .

Wynne pretended to battle her way through clouds of steam in the small but adequate bathroom. 'You sound happy,' she teased. 'Special date?'

Stepping from the shower, Alys wrapped a thick towel about her slim body, face flushed from the heat and the gush of the water and a secret, pulse-quickening anticipation. 'Not really. . .just a friend,' she said airily.

'Well, he's certainly brought a sparkle to your eyes, whoever he is!' Wynne said drily.

Alys smiled. 'What makes you think it's a man?' she countered.

'Was I born yesterday? After the day you've had you'd be curling up in bed with a good book, not worrying what to wear and rushing to get ready to go out with the girls! Is it anyone I know — or shouldn't I ask?'

The teasing tone implied that her friend had a shrewd idea of the identity of her date but was too tactful to point out the risks she ran. Alys wished she knew why she allowed Zachary Howes to sweep aside all her doubts about his reliability with just one smile. . .

Her heart contracted in the oddest manner as he smiled at her across the secluded corner table in an exclusive and probably very expensive restaurant. The excellent food and the heady wine and the warm ambience of their surroundings was making it a memorable evening and she wondered if he felt the same. It was tempting to believe that he did.

He was attentive, at his most charming, making her feel that she was the only woman in his world, and Alys was trying hard to keep her head — and her heart. His was a dangerous charm as he raised his glass in a smiling toast and she feared that its magic might sweep her into his arms without a thought for tomorrow. . .

'Well, what do you think of the Hollywood?' Zack's expansive words and gesture embraced the clever décor and soft lighting. 'Nice, isn't it?'

'It's lovely but I feel a little out of place,' she confessed, looking around her at the beautifully dressed women dining and dancing with men who reeked of inherited wealth or success in their chosen field. 'To be honest, I prefer my own world.'

'With or without Kemp in it?' he ventured, suddenly

needing to know just how much the man mattered to her.

'With *all* my friends in it,' Alys told him firmly.

'I hope my name's on that list.' Zack slid strong fingers over hers, smiling into her slightly guarded eyes.

'I'm not sure that friendship is all you're after!' The teasing words and the sudden smile were more provocative than she knew.

'It paves the way to paradise,' he drawled with a mischievous twinkle

'Don't be so sure!' Warmth swept into her face at the light but meaningful words. 'I've a lot of friends but I'm not planning to explore the paradise you're talking about with any of them just yet!'

She was unused to such a direct approach, Zack decided tenderly as she veiled embarrassed eyes with a sweep of long, thick lashes. Enchanted by the air of innocence that was rare in someone matured by years of nursing, he wondered if she really was the virgin that her words implied.

He didn't like to think of her in the ardent embrace of any man but himself but, looking into the clear, candid pools of her beautiful eyes, Zack knew he didn't care about the past as long as Alys shared some part of the future with him.

Beginning that night. . .

Wrapped in his enclosing arms as they danced, Alys revelled in the male scent of him, the press of his cheek against her hair, the brush of his lips on her temple. He made the lightest of love to her as they moved to the slow, sexy rhythm of an old-fashioned

ballad. Music for lovers — and all that was missing was
the moonlight. Zack provided the magic with the sway
of his body, the strength and security of his arms, the
murmur of his deep voice.

She wondered what had happened to her usually
level head and her sensible heart. She was bewitched
. . .just as the old song was seductively emphasising as
she drifted around the dance-floor in Zack's rhythmic
embrace.

Abruptly clutching at common sense, she drew back
from him. 'Time to go, I think, Zack. It's getting
late. . .'

Zack looked down at her with more than a smile in
the eyes that held her own so compellingly. 'Time to
leave for our own world, anyway,' he agreed softly,
with an implication in his deep, caressing voice that
sent a delicious shiver down her spine.

He kept a protective arm about her shoulders as
they walked towards the car he had parked in a dimly
lit corner of the courtyard. She sat expectantly at his
side as he inserted the key in the ignition and started
the engine, found a music cassette and slotted it into
the player and then turned to smile at her.

Alys was filled with excited anticipation, her heart
hammering so hard and so heavily that she was breathless as he bent his head towards her with unmistakable
intent. The warm pressure of his firm but tender mouth
sent a vibrant, shivering shock through her whole
body, lifting the hair on her head and tingling all the
way to her toes.

The sure, sweet fire of his kiss seared a path to the
very epicentre of her being, evoking a desperate

yearning for more of those magical kisses and his thrilling hands on her body, caressing, exploring, arousing her, a prelude to swooning ecstasy in his arms.

Alys slid both arms about his neck as he kissed her again, instinctively inclining towards him. Quivering and aflame, she wanted him desperately even though she realised that she might just be one more conquest for the sensual SCO.

That night could be a turning-point in her life and, deep down, she wanted it to be this man and no other who took her on that first voyage of discovery on the dark seas of sexual delight. . .

Zack reached for her hands and drew them away from his neck, fired by the sweet yielding of her unexpectedly ardent response, wanting her with an urgency and a passion he had never before felt for any woman but aware that it would be very wrong to take advantage of a wine-influenced mood.

He wanted her to know exactly what she was doing and why when he eventually swept her through the gates of paradise in his arms. . .

As the car came to a stop, Alys sat up and looked at familiar surroundings with a shock of disappointment. She had drowsed against his shoulder as he drove, unaware of the route he was taking through the town. She had told him that she was tired but she hadn't really expected to be taken home so directly!

Flat-sharing could be limiting and both Wynne and Sally grumbled about the lack of privacy at such times. It had never bothered Alys before but at that moment she ardently wanted Zack's kisses, his sensual love-making, his eager embrace drowning all her doubts.

Zack took her heart-shaped face between his strong but sensitive hands and smiled into her eyes. 'It's been a great evening,' he said lightly, as if it had been no different from any other when, in fact, it had made a lasting impression on him. 'We must do it again, Alys.'

'Why not?' she agreed brightly, almost choking on chagrin. She was not so naïve, so totally inexperienced, that she didn't recognise all the signs of a brush-off, she told herself, struggling with hurt at the summary end to the evening. She wondered if he had been abruptly reminded in some way that he owed his loyalty to another woman and the vague shadow that had haunted her throughout the evening suddenly took on a menacing substance. She drew back from his disturbing proximity. 'Do you mean to tell Wanda that you took me out?'

Zack arced an amused eyebrow. 'Do you think I should?' he teased.

Alys shrugged. 'That's a matter for your conscience. I don't know how close you are.'

He frowned at the hint of reproach. 'We aren't close at all—not in the way you mean. You seem to think I'm two-timing her by taking you out. It isn't like that. I've known Wanda all my life. We grew up together. She's a good friend.'

She desperately wanted to believe him but could the juniors be quite so wrong? He might paint Wanda as 'the girl next door' when it suited him but men often married just those girls in the end—and she couldn't forget his admission that he had once proposed to the casualty sister!

'Well, I shall tell Martin,' she said firmly. 'Before someone else does!'

He ran a finger down her cheek in a light caress. 'Why not ask me in for a nightcap and maybe you'll have something more to tell him?' he drawled with a dance of mischief in his smiling eyes, the light words covering his fierce jealousy of her loyal concern for another man's feelings.

She laughed and shook her head. Zack stifled the longing to sweep her close and into willing submission with ardent kisses for she was much too special to be rushed. It wasn't easy to be patient but Alys was surely worth all the waiting. . .and he was prepared to let things take a slow-paced, undemanding course if that was how she wanted it.

Whatever Alys wanted would be right for him. She was the girl he had been waiting all his life to know and love and she had bewitched him completely with her appealing femininity. Zack had never expected to feel so strongly about any woman but he was giving serious thought to the prospect of settling down with this one for the rest of his life.

Fortunately, time was on his side. He could afford to school the urgency of his desire and accept that one last, light kiss to round off the evening was all that she was prepared to allow. . .

Alys resisted the temptation to snuggle into his tall body, to lift her face for another kiss, as he walked her to the foyer with his arm about her waist. She was a confusion of hurt and humiliation for he had aroused newly awakened longings and encouraged her heart to quicken with absurd hope and then left her high and dry and filled with frustration.

Any sensible girl would vow never to have anything more to do with Zachary Howes, she knew. . .

A plate-glass door was opened almost in their faces and Martin confronted them with a blaze of fury in his blue eyes. Startled, Alys moved away from Zack in unconsciously guilty fashion.

'Martin!' she exclaimed in astonishment.

'Didn't expect to see me, did you?' he said coldly, glowering. 'Completely forgot that you were going with me to the civic hall concert, naturally!'

Her eyes widened in shock horror. She *had* forgotten — and it was unforgivable! The tickets had been booked days ago and Martin had talked of little else; Alys herself had been quite excited about the visit of the London Philharmonic Orchestra to the newly opened civic centre in the heart of the town.

'Oh, Martin! I don't know what to say,' she stumbled, embarrassed and contrite.

His expression was grim. 'No need to say anything, is there? The fact that you're with Zack says it all!'

'Hold on, Martin! You can see that Alys genuinely forgot all about the concert and I knew nothing of your plans.' Zack did his best to pour oil on troubled waters although it was obvious that a man who had always regarded him as a rival, both socially and professionally, was in no mood to listen.

'I think you'd better keep out of this!' Martin was obviously struggling to keep his temper, fists clenched and the flush of anger staining his good-looking face as they stood on the pavement outside the tall apartment block, suffused by the security lights. 'You've done your damned best to steal my girl and it looks as if you've succeeded, you bastard! I ought to flatten you. . .!'

CHAPTER TEN

ALYS placed a gently restraining hand on Martin's tensely muscular arm, alarmed by the fury in his good-looking face. 'Fighting won't solve anything — and, besides, it isn't necessary,' she pleaded. 'I'm really sorry I forgot our date but I *can* explain. . .'

'Women think they can explain everything away and make it right,' he said bitterly. 'But you've made a fool of me between you!'

'It isn't like that, Martin! It's been an awful day, dealing with the dead and injured from the accident on the motorway. You must have heard about it! We thought you'd come in to help out but maybe you've been busy?' She tried not to sound as if she was reproaching him. 'It's been chaotic and quite horrific at times — and all thought of the concert went right out of my head, I must admit.'

'I've been to London and knew nothing of the pile-up until tonight. I realised you must have been rushed off your feet but I didn't expect it to affect your memory. I certainly didn't think it necessary to ring and remind you about the concert when we've been talking about it for days!'

Alys had never known him in such a mood or felt the lash of his cutting tongue although she had seen him lose his temper with other people on several occasions. 'I know how it must seem,' she said, dismayed. 'But I didn't deliberately stand you up, Martin. Please believe me.'

Zack scowled. 'You don't have to plead with him, Alys! Let the idiot believe what he likes!'

Blazing with anger, Martin turned on him. 'I warned you, Zack! This has nothing to do with you! Why don't you just get into your flash car and drive away? You've done enough damage for one evening!'

'I've a better idea,' Alys ventured. 'Why don't you both come in for a coffee and we'll sort out this misunderstanding like reasonable people!'

'I'm not in a very reasonable mood at the moment, Alys,' Martin rejected coldly.

'I know you're angry but it isn't Zack's fault!' she protested. 'There's no need to vent your annoyance on him.'

'I *am* angry and with good reason. He's been making a dead set at you — and you've fallen for it!'

'All's fair in love and war,' Zack drawled with a cool smile that infuriated Martin even more.

'Love is the last thing on *your* mind. . .and if Alys has any sense she knows it!'

It was her turn to be angry — and partly because she had a horrid suspicion that Martin could be right. 'I wish you'd stop snarling at each other like two dogs wanting the same bone,' she said sharply. 'I'm beginning to feel sorry that I ever went out with either of you!'

She left them on that surge of irritation, thrusting through the heavy doors into the foyer. With her back to the two men, Alys didn't see who struck the first

blow but she glanced round to see Martin on the
ground and Zack standing over him.

About to shrug slim shoulders and leave them to it,
impatient with the male conviction that most things
could be settled with their fists, she saw Zack's
expression change from anger to alarm as he bent over
Martin's still recumbent frame.

Instantly, she hurried back with a flurry of floating
skirts and flying curls. Zack was crouching beside
Martin, trained fingers instinctively seeking a pulse, an
anxious frown touching his steel-grey eyes.

'What is it? Is he all right?' Careless of her white
skirts and delicate stockings, Alys fell to her knees
beside the unconscious CO, horrified to see blood
streaming from the back of his head.

'I didn't hit him that hard. . .' Zack shook his head
in astonishment.

'You shouldn't have hit him at all!' she flared
protectively.

'A man's entitled to defend himself.'

She glowered. 'You must have said something to
provoke him!'

'Not at all. I merely pointed out that he doesn't own
you and we'd spent a perfectly innocent evening over
a meal and a bottle of wine.' He looked down at her
straightly. 'I'm sure you wouldn't want me to repeat
what he said about you, Alys. He's bloody lucky that I
kept my temper.'

'If this is the result of keeping your temper then I'm
very thankful you didn't lose it!' She thrust a hand
inside Martin's shirt to check for the throb of his heart,

anxiety increasing as he showed no sign of stirring. 'He ought to be coming round by now, surely?'

Zack checked the pupils of Martin's closed eyes. 'Perhaps we should get him to Casualty,' he said soberly. 'I don't like the look of him.'

'Isn't that why you hit him?' Alys returned coldly, bitingly sarcastic.

He frowned. 'I appreciate your concern for your boyfriend but verbal attacks on me won't improve the situation!'

She shrugged off the rebuke in his tone. 'I think he's badly hurt. . .' She continued to stanch the blood with a wad of tissues from her bag.

'He cracked his head on the ground when he went down. There may be some serious damage,' Zack admitted. 'You'd better call an ambulance, Alys.'

'Shouldn't I call the police, too?' Upset that an impulsive acceptance of an invitation had led to such an awful outcome, Alys vented the turmoil of her feelings on Zack with the caustic words.

She hated violence, having seen far too much of its results in the weeks she had spent in A and E, and she deplored the fact that two responsible doctors whose daily lives were spent in treating the victims of accidents or vicious attack had come to blows in such fashion and for so little cause.

'For God's sake, Alys. . .!' Zack felt quite bad enough without that threat. Hopefully, there would be no need to involve the law—but Kemp was certainly taking a hell of a time to recover from a light blow to the chin. It should have floored him and given him second thoughts about the way he had slandered Alys, but this lengthy blackout was both unexpected and worrying.

Zack hoped it was nothing more than a slight concussion. . .

X-rays confirmed the deep-down fear of a hairline fracture and Martin was admitted to a side-ward in the neurosurgical unit for treatment and observation.

Despite reassuring noises from the duty neurosurgeon before he went away, Zack studied the X-ray plates in the illuminated rack with a drawn look to his handsome face and a grim set to his mobile mouth, sure that he faced the prospect of being charged with assault at best and grievous bodily harm at worst.

Alys entered the unit office with a mug of steaming coffee in each hand. 'Sally suggested I use the ward kitchen to make us both a hot drink,' she said as he glanced at her in surprise. Newly transferred to the NSU and senior staff nurse on duty that night, her friend probably suspected what had happened between the two doctors that night but she hadn't asked questions.

'Thanks. . . I need that,' he said gratefully.

She was very worried about Martin in spite of assurances that his condition wasn't critical. But she didn't have the thought of possible prosecution hanging over her head and her anger melted when she saw Zack's troubled face and slumped figure. She knew she would find no satisfaction in reviling him when he was so anxious about the consequences of an unlucky blow.

'Why don't you go home, Zack? You're on duty

again tomorrow and you should get some sleep,' she urged.

He marvelled at her failure to understand the seriousness of his position. 'Do you really think that it will be business as usual for me? You don't seem to realise that this could mean the end of everything, Alys. Job, career prospects—and possibly even my licence to practise medicine!'

Alys studied him with a sober light in her hazel eyes. 'And I'm to blame.'

'No! I hit the poor devil!' he reminded her wearily, having no wish to shift any of the blame to her innocent shoulders.

'Only you and I know that—and I haven't said anything,' she assured him swiftly.

His eyes narrowed. 'What *have* you said?' he asked abruptly. 'Our stories need to match, Alys!'

'That you were just sparring and caught him on the chin by accident and he hit his head as he went down. Do you think I want the world to know what really happened? No, thanks, Zack! I think Sergeant Moss believed me, anyway. . .'

The beat policeman had visited A and E that night to investigate the stabbing of a pusher by a local drug addict. Alys had seen his comfortably rounded figure in the reception area and seized the opportunity to ask his advice while Martin's X-rays were being studied by the casualty officer on duty.

Making light of the argument and Martin's resultant injury, she stressed that he and Zack were really the best of friends as well as colleagues and that both their careers would be affected if the matter went to court.

The police sergeant was a regular visitor to A and E, often called to deal with difficult or disturbed patients, and he had assured her that the authorities weren't interested in private quarrels if someone who had come off worst in an exchange of blows didn't choose to press charges.

'I'm sure that Dr Kemp won't want to take things that far,' Alys had declared, more confidently than she felt. 'The doctors say he'll be fully recovered in a few weeks. It would be a tragedy if Dr Howes was struck off because of a disagreement with a friend — and I just know that it's the last thing Martin would want!'

'This Dr Howes is a lucky man to have a pretty girl like you to plead his case for him,' the sergeant had said, smiling. 'I don't think you need to worry, Nurse. If no official complaint has been made, then I think you can safely assume that matters won't go any further. Unless there's a possibility that the young man might die from his injuries, of course.'

She had shuddered. 'That isn't at all likely, thank heavens!' she had exclaimed with feeling and hurried away to find Zack and put his mind at rest.

Now, she perched on the edge of the desk in her white silk dress with its gold-embroidered bodice and the floating skirts that had suffered somewhat from contact with the wet and muddy ground and repeated some of that unofficial conversation with Sergeant Moss.

Halfway through the recital, Sally stuck her head into the room. 'Martin's come round! He feels groggy, naturally — and complains of a headache, which isn't

surprising! You can see him for a few minutes but try
not to tire him. . .'

Alys saw Zack's sombre expression lighten at the
news. 'Oh, that *is* a relief!' she exclaimed gladly.
'Thanks, Sally! I just want to see for myself that he's
all right and then I'll leave him to rest, I promise!' As
her friend hurried away, she turned to Zack. 'That
must be a weight off your mind.'

He nodded. 'It's too early to be sure that there'll be
no lasting effects but the damage seems to be minimal
and John Winter says the prognosis is good. You do
know that I didn't mean to hurt him that badly, don't
you, Alys?'

'Perhaps not but there was no need to add injury to
insult!' she said coolly, far from ready to relent in spite
of the flooding relief. 'I think you'd better go home,
Zack. I mean to make tracks for home and bed myself
shortly.' She smothered a huge yawn. 'It's been an
eventful night. . .'

It hadn't ended in the way that she had wistfully
hoped and she wasn't inclined to forgive Zack. It was
dreadful that two grown men should quarrel over her
as if she were a desirable object! If Martin had suffered
brain damage or lasting paralysis as a result, she could
never have forgiven herself. But at least the incident
had clarified her feelings, she decided. She wanted
nothing more to do with Dr Zachary Howes! In future,
she would limit her love life to Martin—much safer
and holding far more promise for the future than
hankering for a man she couldn't trust not to play fast
and loose with her heart!

'I'll wait until you've seen Martin and then take you

home, Alys.' Zack realised even as he spoke that she would refuse. Whatever had briefly flickered between them had been crushed into extinction in a moment. He had only defended himself from yet another physical assault by a jealous colleague but he doubted that Alys would believe him or even listen to his side of the story.

'I think we've given people enough to talk about without leaving together in the dead of night,' she announced firmly.

Zack shrugged. 'Just as you wish.' Unused to rebuff or the feelings that Alys evoked so strongly, he sounded harsh and uncaring when in fact he cared far more than he wanted her or anyone else to know.

Even a man in love held on to his pride, he was discovering, perhaps to his cost. . .

Alys looked after him as he strode towards the lifts. He was anxious to get away and she didn't really blame him. Seeing the speaking dejection of his broad back, she almost relented and ran to put her comforting arms about him.

Instead, she packed ice more firmly about her heart. She had probably made too many mistakes already where Zachary Howes was concerned. . .

Martin winced with pain as he turned his head to look at her as Alys sat down beside the bed. She knew better than to encourage him to talk but she did her best to convey remorse and caring concern with her smile and soft words of comfort. As he closed his eyes on a sigh that she interpreted as one of satisfaction, she decided that he just wanted to know that she was there.

She would be there for him for as long as he wanted her, she decided impulsively. Martin was the kind of man she felt she could trust with her happiness. Who needed Zachary Howes with his careless disregard for the feelings of the peace of mind of the unsuspecting women he encouraged to care for him?

Alys went in search of Sally before she left the NSU. The main ward was hushed and dimly lit, most patients sleeping and the night staff going quietly about their chores. A patient's cough or groan sounded louder than it was, the occasional call of alarm or anxiety echoing throughout the near-silent room.

It was some time since she had worked on the wards at night but she remembered how different it was from daytime nursing. Sick people lay awake, fretful and burdened with anxieties that they could sometimes be coaxed to pour into a sympathetic ear, and many confidences were exchanged between the hard-working nurses during the long night hours.

Sally was writing up her report but she looked up with a smile as Alys approached the nursing station.

'He *is* going to be all right,' she said gently, sensing her friend's mix of guilt, concern and dismay. Alys was more transparent than she knew and both Wynne and herself had observed her increasing interest in Zachary Howes and her retreat into Martin's welcoming arms.

'I know—but I feel dreadful,' Alys sighed. 'I shouldn't have forgotten that I'd promised to go out with him tonight—and I certainly shouldn't have let Zack talk me into having dinner with him!'

'Then what happened wasn't really an accident?'

Sally's quiet, unsurprised tone encouraged her long-time friend to unburden herself and Alys leaned on the desk and propped her head on her hand as a wave of weariness swept over her.

'No. According to Wynne, Martin had waited in the flat all evening for me to come home. When he saw Zack's car drive up with me in the passenger seat at his side, he rushed out to confront him. They exchanged a few insults and I left them to it. When I looked back, I saw they'd exchanged blows, too—and Martin was out cold! But please don't let it go any further, Sally!' she beseeched.

'Of course I won't,' her friend said warmly, understanding her dread of grapevine gossip.

'I don't want everyone to know that *I* was the cause of Martin getting hurt!'

'I wouldn't care to be in your shoes if Wanda Nelson hears the real version of events!' Sally said drily. 'You are an idiot, Alys. I thought you were so sure that you didn't like Zachary Howes enough to go anywhere with him! Oh, I know! He's got it all—looks, charm, sex appeal. I expect *I'd* leap at the chance if he ever wanted to take me out—Wanda or no Wanda!'

'I'm not interested in what she thinks. My concern is for Martin. He was so hurt and I feel as if I've let him down.'

'He seems to be very fond of you.' Just like most people at Benny's, she had been misled by the CO's apparent interest in her friend.

Alys sighed. 'I know—and I'm fond of him, too. But I'm not ready to commit myself in the way he seems to expect. Frankly, I just can't see myself setting up home and having kids and growing old with Martin. . .'

Her wilful fancy promptly conjured up a vision of a happy home with herself and Zack in it, a boy in his image and a girl looking like herself — and she hastily pushed away such an unlikely fantasy.

'Then you're certainly not in love with him,' Sally said shrewdly.

'No — and I don't want him to be in love with me! I ought to stop dating him, to be fair. But I can't ditch him after what's happened! Not right away, anyway. He'd think I cared more for Zack than for him — and, even worse, Zack would think so, too!'

'And you *don't* care for Zack,' Sally sympathised, keeping her private thoughts to herself. She and Wynne had agreed ages ago that Alys protested a little too much about her indifference to the good-looking SCO.

'No! Of course I don't. I'd be a fool, wouldn't I? A man like Zachary Howes!' Alys retorted sharply. 'By all accounts, he's been working his way through a long list of women for years!'

'Looking for his one true love, perhaps?' Sally suggested lightly.

Alys snorted. 'If you believe the grapevine, he's found her in Wanda Nelson — and the rest of us are just helping him to pass the time until she eventually relents and agrees to marry him! I wish she would! Then perhaps we can all get on with our lives without having to fend him off!'

She almost meant the fiery words. But she did mean

to snub Zack if he showed the slightest degree of
interest in her in future. She had learned her lesson —
fortunately before she burned her fingers badly at the
flame of attraction!

CHAPTER ELEVEN

As ALYS let herself into the apartment, Wynne leaped out of bed, unable to settle since the ambulance had left for Benny's with siren wailing.

Martin had insisted on waiting when he found that Alys had gone out for the evening, becoming more and more agitated as the hours passed, and finally had bolted from the flat at the sound of the car. Minutes later, watching from the apartment window, she had witnessed the sudden, unprovoked attack on the SCO and its outcome and rushed to do what she could.

'How's Martin?' she asked anxiously, appearing at her bedroom door in her dressing-gown and belting it about a waist that would never be as trim as her friend's for all the weight-watching.

'He's come round, thank goodness. It isn't too bad . . .a hairline fracture and three stitches. But he'll be out of action for a few weeks. . .' Alys ran her fingers through her tousled curls and plumped herself heavily on the sofa cushions, eyes gritty and every bone in her body aching. She was very near to tears. 'Oh, Wynne—why can't I resist Zachary Howes when I don't even like him?' she wailed on a sudden collapse of her defences.

Wynne perched on the arm of the sofa and put a comforting arm about her shoulders. 'He's a very sexy man,' she said sagely.

'Yes—and that's all it is, I know. Just sex. . .' Alys
instantly seized on a more acceptable explanation for
the way she felt about Zack than the dreadful possibility that she had fallen headlong into love with him.

'Don't underestimate the powers of physical attraction,' Wynne warned. 'It's made trouble for people
since time began—Adam and Eve included!'

Alys smiled wanly. 'I just wish he'd leave me alone.'
She was too tired to realise how much she gave away
with the bewildered look in her eyes.

'You must be giving him the come-on, whether you
realise it or not. . .and you aren't exactly refusing to
get involved, are you?'

'Well, I won't get involved again!'

The next morning, Alys hurried down the stone
stairs that led from the neurosurgical unit, uniform
skirts flying and her haste threatening the perch of the
starched cap on her thick curls, having spent longer
than she intended with Martin and rushing to avoid a
rebuke for arriving late for duty.

She wasn't looking forward to her first moments
with Wanda, who must have already heard the full
story from Zack and would have no hesitation in laying
the blame squarely on *her* shoulders.

Rounding a corner, she almost collided with the
SCO and they both came to a dead stop. Alys tensed
and the hand he had almost reached out to her fell
back to his side as he saw the recoil in her expressive
eyes.

'I've just been to see Martin. . .'

'I'm on my way to see Martin. . .'

They spoke together, broke off together, and then

Zack smiled, a little wryly. 'Is there any change?' Hurt by her look of dismay at their surprise encounter on the stairs, he reminded himself that he hadn't expected her to be pleased to see him again, in the circumstances.

'He had a bad night and isn't very well this morning. Feels sick.' Her tone was crisply formal, tinkling with ice.

'Who doesn't?' he said briefly.

He looked like a man who hadn't slept at all but Alys hardened the heart that threatened to melt merely for seeing him. 'At least you don't have to worry about your job. Martin doesn't know how fit he'll be when he gets over this,' she told him sharply.

'John Winter seems fairly confident that there won't be any problem on that score.' Zack tried to ignore the censure in her tone.

'As long as there aren't any complications in the next few days!'

'You don't have to work at making me feel bad, Alys,' he told her quietly.

'There's really no point in talking about it, is there?' Alys fled before she softened.

Zack continued soberly on his way to the NSU. He would need to be blind or stupid not to understand the situation, he felt. An age-old attraction had briefly sparked between Alys and himself but she meant to stay out of his arms in future.

It was only now, left with a shattered dream, that he realised how firmly he had set his heart on winning her—and his bitter disappointment had little to do with frustrated desire. He wanted her with all the force

of his very sensual nature but his feelings had deepened and set, going way beyond the merely physical.

Love had invaded his heart and his life like a
thunderbolt. . .

'Late again, Nurse Mackenzie!'

Alys flinched from the cold dislike in the casualty
sister's dark eyes. 'I'm sorry, Sister. I went straight to
the NSU. Information is so unsatisfactory and I felt I
just had to see for myself how Dr Kemp is this
morning.'

'Wishing he'd never met you, I imagine,' Wanda
returned scathingly, consumed with dislike and a bitter
jealousy of the girl who had apparently won the heart
that had refused to warm to her love for Martin. 'I
suppose you know that the entire hospital is talking
about what happened last night!'

'The entire hospital doesn't *know* what happened
last night!' Alys realised that she should have known
better than to expect any sympathy or understanding
from the casualty sister! 'I dare say Zack's given you
his version and you're only too ready to believe it!'

'He told me that you spent the evening with him, if
that's what you mean. I can't say I blame Dr Kemp for
objecting,' Wanda said coldly. 'It's a pity you didn't
heed what I said to you the other day!'

Alys looked back at her steadily. 'I'm not sure if
you're furious because I went out with Zack or because
Martin was hurt as a result. I wish you'd make it clear
which one it is you really want and we'd all know
where we stand!'

Aware that Alys misunderstood her long-time
friendship with Zack and wasn't sure of his feelings,

too jealous to care if she angered Zack as long as she
punished the girl for behaviour that had put Martin
into a hospital bed, Wanda lashed out blindly with the
intent to hurt.

'I can certainly tell you that Zack is in no doubt at
all where *he* stands—or what he wants,' she said
cuttingly. 'Just because he couldn't resist a blatant
invitation you mustn't assume that you're something
special. It's time you knew that there's only one
woman he's ever cared about—and that's me!'

'And that pleases you?' Alys countered hotly,
incensed by the smug tone and dismayed by the words
that confirmed her own deep-down anxiety. 'I suppose
it suits your vanity to keep him dangling on a string
although you don't really want him! Perhaps you need
him around to save your face because the man you *do*
want isn't interested any more!'

Wanda's mouth tightened into a thin line. Her eyes
were glowing coals of angry dislike in a pale, pinched
face, its venom cancelling out her claim to beauty. She
could forgive almost anything but having her authority
undermined in front of junior nurses and medical
clerks and a number of patients who stared and
blatantly strained their ears to listen to the low, angry
words.

'How dare you speak to me in that tone, Nurse
Mackenzie? Go and get on with your work and I'll see
you in my office later.' She stalked away with hard
eyes smouldering in a stony face.

'You've made an enemy there,' Nicola murmured as
she scanned the chalked list of patients still waiting in

curtained cubicles for attention on yet another busy morning. 'If looks could kill. . .'

Alys shrugged. 'She's never liked me.'

'She's a very jealous woman. Be on your guard,' Nicola advised. 'She'll be out for revenge in one way or another.'

'There isn't much she can do, is there? I'm not a bad nurse and she can't complain about my work.'

She sounded insouciant but she knew there were several means the casualty sister could use to remove her from A and E — and as far as possible from Zack.

And perhaps they both needed to be out of the reach of temptation. . .

'You're a very good nurse,' Nicola agreed with her friendly smile. 'And your excellent qualities are needed right now,' she added with a meaningful glance at the rapidly filling benches.

Taking the hint, Alys hurried away to usher a limping girl into an empty cubicle. Guided by years of nursing experience, she did a cursory examination of a badly swollen ankle and made a tentative diagnosis. 'It's probably just a bad sprain but I'll ask Doctor to look at it. . .' she said brightly to reassure the patient, but privately thought it more than that.

X-rays showed a fracture of a small bone just below the ankle and Alys was given the job of strapping up the girl's foot. Then she nursed a screaming toddler with a temperature while Nicola did her best to examine him and make a diagnosis before admitting him to the children's ward for observation.

Throughout a succession of minor cuts and bruises and scalds, she waited for the expected summons to

the office and eventually decided that the casualty
sister had thought better of open confrontation.

Alys welcomed the busyness of the day for it left
few moments to worry about Martin or to recall the
disturbing look in Zack's eyes as she ran from that
brief encounter on the stairs. She kept out of his way
as much as possible and he didn't seek an opportunity
to speak to her, apparently more preoccupied with
soothing Wanda's ruffled feathers and seemingly the
only person who could bring a smile to that coldly
beautiful face.

That evening, Alys was just about to go off duty
when an ambulance brought in an infant who had been
briefly left alone in the bath while his mother went for
an airing towel. Longer than she had intended because
she'd paused to answer a ringing telephone, the dis-
traught girl had found her baby face down in the water
on her return. The paramedics had revived him during
the siren-screaming race through busy town streets but
his heart stopped again as they rushed him into A and
E.

Hastily setting out a tracheotomy kit, Alys assisted
the team with the desperate attempt at rescuscitation,
her gaze concentrated on Zack's clever hands as he
worked tirelessly on his small patient, the child's frail
form and tiny limbs and bloodless appearance tearing
at her heart. After thirty minutes of unavailing effort,
he was forced to admit defeat, and she fought the scald
of tears as he stood back from the small victim of a
needless tragedy with a sad shake of his head.

She grieved for the prematurely snuffed-out life as
nurses took down drips and removed tubes and

detached the electrodes connecting the small body to the silent monitor. Putting her arms about the numbed and disbelieving mother, she led her away, knowing there was little that anyone could say to comfort someone who'd lost a child so tragically.

Her heart-shaped face was solemn and her hazel eyes held the glint of unshed tears as she made her way to the changing-room some time later. Nursing, with its many glimpses of private traumas and trage-dies, was almost too painful to bear at times and she wondered if she should give it up. Training and dedi-cation seemed to count for very little when they couldn't save such a precious young life, she mourned.

'We work a lot of miracles,' Zack said softly, catch-ing up with her and reading her troubled thoughts in that very expressive face. 'Perhaps the occasional failure is meant to remind us that we can't always play God.'

'My heart bleeds for that poor girl,' she admitted heavily.

'She knows. It showed—and it helped as much as anything can right now. Try not to dwell on it too much, Alys. We can only do our best.'

She saw from his shadowed eyes that he was sorely feeling his own inadequacy. He cared deeply about every one of his patients and dedicated his life to their problems. He was a good, kind and genuinely caring man—and she suddenly realised with a shocked thump of her heart just how much she loved him.

With a brief, comforting pat of her shoulder, Zack swung away down the corridor, and she looked after him in dismay at the unexpected thawing and surrender of her heart to a man who was never likely to love her in return. . .

Both Zack and Wanda were off duty for the rest of the week and Alys did her best to close her mind to the thought of how they might be spending the days — and nights — but she couldn't close her ears to the rumour that they were busy with wedding plans. It seemed to her troubled heart and mind that Zack's scheme had worked and he had got what he really wanted — and that Wanda had finally made up her mind which of the two men *she* wanted!

Alys went about her work with a heavy heart, spending as much time as possible with Martin, unaware that her affectionate concern was encouraging him to believe that she cared for him.

The rumours about Zack's and Wanda's marriage plans eventually reached his ears, too, dismaying him more than he wanted to admit. Anxious to protect his pride, determined to show Wanda that he was unaffected by her sudden decision to marry his long-time rival, he crushed the surprising surge of jealousy and made up his mind to court Alys in earnest. She was a lovely girl and he was very fond of her and he felt he could trust her not to make too many demands on him.

'I don't expect you to spend every moment of your precious off-duty hours with me, you know,' he said one afternoon, a thumb ceaselessly caressing her imprisoned hand. 'There must be lots of other things you want to be doing.'

Alys felt trapped by his obvious dependence on her affection and support. It was wrong to let him think they had a future together yet she couldn't undeceive him at this stage. 'I want to be here,' she declared brightly. 'It's the least I can do. . .'

'And I'm glad to have you here. . .as long as you're sure you wouldn't rather be somewhere else?'

With someone else, she knew he meant, and stifled the wish that followed the thought. 'Of course not. . .' She leaned to kiss him lightly on the cheek.

It was an almost obsessive conversation, constantly repeated, and it became increasingly hard to be patient and reassuring. John Winter said it was just the temporary effect of a traumatic blow to the head but Alys was sure it was more than that. For all her efforts at reassurance, Martin obviously sensed that she still hankered for a man who no longer wanted her at all, and felt that his happiness was threatened, she told herself heavily.

Perhaps it was because her spirits were at such a low ebb that she agreed to Martin's proposal of marriage. At least, she supposed she had said yes to him although she couldn't recall doing so, she realised with a shock when her friends offered congratulations. It was much more likely that he had taken her startled silence for agreement but it seemed such a sensible solution to the dismaying muddle of her emotions that she decided to let it stand. . .

Her mother's first reaction was one of delight. 'Oh, I liked him very much! I really couldn't wish for anyone better for you, Alys.'

'Martin's a dear,' she agreed.

'And you love him,' Marian prompted, smiling.

Naturally honest, Alys hesitated. 'I can trust him not to let me down,' she said finally.

Marian studied her, seeking in vain the glow of happiness, the misty dreams, that she expected to find in the eyes of a woman in love.

'Marriage isn't easy even when two people love each other dearly,' she warned. 'Trust and liking are fine but not enough when so much is at stake. *Do* you love him, Alys?'

'You married for love and it didn't work out. I'm not convinced that it's the best basis for marriage,' Alys returned defensively.

'It really doesn't sound as if you should rush into anything.' Concern touched her mother's tone.

'Don't worry, Mum. I know what I'm doing.'

'Well, just be very sure that you want to spend the rest of your life with Martin, that's all.'

Alys shook her head to the offer of another cup of coffee. 'That was a lovely meal, Mum. But I must get back. I'm on duty early in the morning. . .'

Marian got to her feet. 'It's time for the evening round, anyway. . .and I want to look in on one of our ladies. She's eighty-two and she has Alzheimer's— only in its early stages as yet but she gets confused and tends to wander about in the middle of the night.' Ushering Alys from her comfortable sitting-room, she went on, 'She used to be a nanny and she thinks she's checking on her charges, poor old thing. She has a visitor tonight. Someone she cared for when he was a child, but I'm afraid she doesn't really know who he is. It's very sad. . .'

As they made their way to the main hall, a tall man

with dark, crisply curling hair and lean good looks emerged from a resident's room with one of the care attendants. Heart leaping wildly in her breast, Alys did her best to conceal the start of delighted surprise. 'Nanny's visitor, presumably,' she murmured.

Marian glanced round. 'Oh, yes. . . Dr Howes. I knew his parents years ago. That's why I agreed to such a late visit. He's very good with Ellie Summers, encourages her to remember things. I believe he works at Benny's,' she added, having observed her daughter's betraying confusion. 'Perhaps you know him?'

Alys knew a denial was pointless. Zack would take a delight in discomfiting her, she felt. 'He's our SCO,' she admitted reluctantly.

'Then of course you know him well. . .oh, Dr Howes!' As Zack approached, Marian turned to him, her likeness to her daughter evident in the impulsive warmth of her smile. 'How is Miss Summers this evening?'

'She was rather tired but I managed to make her understand that I was young Master Zachary — and got thoroughly scolded for climbing on to the roof of the stables to rescue an injured bird.' He smiled in wry understanding of the old lady's problems. 'I'd forgotten the incident — and the outcome, so it was nice to be reminded that the bird survived my immature first aid. She has a remarkable memory for the past even if she is a little patchy about the present.'

'I'm sure she was stimulated by your visit. She talks so much about you that she must have been very fond of you,' Marian said warmly.

'I didn't know it at the time. My sister was always

her favourite. . .' His face clouded. 'She asked for Jenny but I didn't feel it would do her any good to be told that she'd died.'

'She must have been a rather elderly nanny,' Alys said stiffly, wondering how he would react to the news that she was engaged to Martin.

'She was the family nanny, persuaded to come out of retirement when my mother's political career took off. Jenny and I couldn't have had a better or more loving person to take care of us.'

Alys was suddenly choked with emotion. Perhaps it was the mention of his dead sister or his obvious affection for an old lady or simply the rush of regret that she had promised to marry Martin when something deep down inside her clamoured for a lifetime of loving with a man who had not only taught her the meaning of passion but also melted the ice about her cautious heart. . .

CHAPTER TWELVE

THE perceptive Marian Mackenzie stepped into the breach, giving her daughter time to master emotions she recognised from her own experience of loving, rather relieved that Alys wasn't as cold-hearted as she pretended and suddenly understanding the lack of expected delight in an engagement she had probably entered into for all the wrong reasons.

'I remember your mother very well,' she said brightly. 'I was in charge of her ward when she had surgery for a breast cancer. As a socialist MP, she insisted on National Health treatment. She was very brave and an inspiration to all the other patients.'

From his towering height, Zack smiled down at the diminutive woman. 'My father has told me about your devoted nursing and how kind you were.'

'He was the devoted one!' Marian exclaimed with remembered admiration. 'Scarcely left your mother's side — and those were the days when visiting hours were strictly regulated. I had rather a soft spot for him and sometimes turned a blind eye when he remained after the bell had been rung.'

'He asked me to give you his best wishes.' Zack didn't add that he had talked to his father about Sister Wells's pretty daughter, too, possibly the first time he had enlarged on any woman in his life and certain to give rise to the suspicion that he had marriage in mind.

144

So he had—even if the woman he wanted to marry was engaged to another man!

He didn't want to believe that Alys was irrevocably committed. Knowing her tender heart, he felt sure that she had found it impossible to refuse Martin because she felt responsible for his accident. All very foolish but understandable and, given the least sign that she regretted the engagement that had given him such a shock on hearing the news, he would extricate her from it with all speed!

'I'll leave you to reminisce. . .' Alys wafted a kiss across her mother's cheek. 'I really must run if I'm to catch the last bus!'

'My car's outside,' Zack said promptly. 'Let me run you home, Alys. . .'

'I couldn't impose on you,' she demurred but her heart fluttered at the prospect of his company for as long as it took to drive into town from the nursing home in its pleasant but isolated rural setting.

'Darling, if Dr Howes is kind enough to offer a lift then don't offend him by refusing,' Marian said firmly. 'You know I don't like you travelling alone late at night.'

'It's only half-past nine,' Alys protested lightly. 'I'll be fine. . .'

'Your daughter has such an independent streak that it isn't easy to do things for her, I'm afraid.' Zack smiled at Alys as she stiffened. 'You'll be doing me the favour, believe me. I nearly got lost on my way here and I need you to direct me back to the town. . .'

'What a tale!' Alys reproached as Zack ushered her towards his car with a caring hand at her elbow. 'Lost

your way and need me to guide you home, indeed!'
But her eyes smiled at him as she uttered the mocking
words for her heart hummed happily at his wish for
her company.

'I'm a stranger in these parts,' he assured her, mock-
serious.

She cast him a sceptical glance. 'I'm sure you are —
growing up with your sister less than a mile away! Isn't
that house at the top of Lowley Hill where your
parents live?' she challenged.

'They do now. But when I was a boy we lived about
six miles out in the other direction — Fenleigh. It was
just a village then. Now it's a vast housing estate for
the overspill of newcomers since the town expanded.
But it's true enough that my parents live in the area
now,' he went on lightly. 'We could call on them, if
you like. I'd like you to meet them.'

'I don't mean to seem rude but I'd rather not,' she
said carefully, her heart plunging with disappointment
that there was no point in meeting his parents. How
gladly she would have agreed if there had been the
least hope that they might welcome her as a daughter-
in-law one day!

'They would be thrilled to meet the daughter of
Sister Wells,' Zack told her with his warm smile. 'I
wonder if you realise how much your mother meant to
so many people. Her warm heart and sweet nature
apparently made a lasting impact on her patients.' His
smile deepened. 'You're very like her, you know.'

Warmth stole into her face at the quiet compliment
of the words but she kept her gaze firmly fixed on the
winding ribbon of road for she knew she would be

totally lost if she looked into the inviting depths of his eyes with their power to sway her heart as well as her senses.

'I'd like to think I *am* like my mother but it's hard trying to live up to such a model,' she said lightly. 'From my very first day at Benny's, I've been told what a marvellous ward sister she was and how much the patients loved her. Now she's turned Link Lodge into a real home for its elderly residents.' She glanced at him curiously, wondering what had taken him to the nursing home that evening. 'Doesn't your mother visit her old nanny? It seems more likely that she should than *you*, frankly.'

'She's been away for a couple of weeks, canvassing for local elections, and only came home this morning. But she knows exactly where and how Nanny Summers is — and I was happy to volunteer as a proxy visitor. I wanted to meet *your* mother, for one thing.'

'Oh. . .!' Alys was surprised and showed it.

A smile hovered about his sensual mouth. 'She's a delightful person. What does she think about your absurd engagement, by the way?'

She stiffened but few secrets could be kept in a large general hospital, particularly as Martin had blurted out the news to Sally almost immediately. It was probably common knowledge by now!

'I don't know why you think it's so absurd!' she exclaimed, stung by the mocking tone with its total lack of concern or dismay. 'It's a natural thing to happen when two people care about each other!'

Zack brought the car to a sudden halt on the quiet country road and Alys felt a flurry of alarm mixed with a tingling excitement as he turned his powerful body towards her.

'*This* is a natural thing to happen when two people care about each other,' he said firmly, taking her into strong, secure arms and capturing her soft, startled lips with his confident kiss.

Her heart trembled at the mastery of his mouth and the command of his embrace. His kiss was magical, transporting her to a world where no one and nothing mattered but his mouth on her own, his hands on her body, and she quivered with longing as his kiss deepened with sensual promise.

Breathless, filled with a tumultuous desire, she clung to him, past caring if she told him all too plainly how much she loved him, and Zack held her to his heart, a hint of the triumphant male in the glow of his grey eyes, making her feel that she was the one woman he wanted more than any other in the world.

Even if it was only true for one night. . .

Regretfully, Zack released her. 'I refuse to make love to you here,' he averred. 'I think we deserve better than the front or back seat of a car, however luxurious, don't you, my sweet? Your place or mine?' The self-mocking tone and the teasing twinkle in his eyes as he murmured the hackneyed words evoked the smile he had hoped. 'Mine, I think, don't you?'

Alys suspected that he would sweep aside the reminder that she was supposed to be engaged to Martin. Particularly as he obviously knew just as well as she did that nothing would keep her out of his arms that night.

Promising to marry Martin had been a mistake that

she must put right as soon as possible. In the meantime, her whole being craved the ecstasy that Zack promised with his smile and a tender kiss before he set the car in motion once more.

Nevertheless, she felt a return of doubt mingled with a tingling apprehension once she was over the threshold of his male abode and surrounded by the modern décor, expensive leather furnishings and the personal possessions that revealed more about the man she had so unexpectedly come to love.

'Perhaps you should take me home, after all,' she said unsteadily, feeling vulnerable, knowing that the intimacy of lovemaking would set the seal on the feeling that she couldn't bear to live the rest of her life without him.

Sensitive to her uncertainty, Zack put an arm about her slim shoulders and drew her towards him. 'If that's really what you want—sure! In a while. But first let's get to know each other a little better, Alys.' His lips were soft and reassuring as they brushed her cheek and then her hair. 'There's so much I want to know about you, darling—and I'd like you to learn that there's much more to me than an undeserved reputation for chasing nurses!'

Heartened by the gentle endearment and the promise of patience, Alys relaxed, feeling she should have known that someone so caring would give her time to be really sure.

Zack put on some music and opened a bottle of wine and they sat in comfortable companionship, talking books and films and mutual friends, and Alys found out more about him in that hour than she had

learned in two months of working with him and felt
that he admitted her to his lasting friendship with the
relaxing of his usual reserve.

Sitting at his side on the deep-cushioned sofa, listening to his deep voice and studying the play of
expressions across his handsome face, she loved him
more than ever and felt a frenzied impatience to know
his arms about her and his kisses sweeping her to the
heaven she could only find in his embrace. Drawn by
desire, she put a hand on his muscular forearm in a
tentative caress and smiled as he turned to her.

Promptly putting down his glass, he caught and
gripped her slender fingers so fiercely that they felt
bruised. 'Don't smile at me with that look in your eyes
unless you really mean what they're saying,' he
warned, husky-voiced, urgent with love and longing.

She moistened dry lips with the pink tip of her
tongue, innocently provocative. 'Perhaps I'll be sure
that I mean it if you kiss me, Zack. . .'

He brushed the shining wisps of hair from her
temple, caressed the delicate ear, the arcing eyebrow
and the frail eyelid, stroked the soft silk of her cheek
and the sweet curve of her mouth before his lips
tenderly followed the route his fingers had traced.

As Alys sighed with content and put an arm about
his neck, his hand slid lower to the velvet of her throat
and the delicious swell of her breasts and she held her
breath, heart pounding and body melting at his slow,
sure touch. He unfastened buttons and drew aside the
lacy covering, strong hand curving reverently about
the tender mound of her breast. As he lowered his
head to kiss its proud peak, the fierce flame of love

and longing coursed through her veins and she sensed
his taut desire, the urgency of a need far more powerful than her own because he already knew what lay
beyond the gates of paradise.

Eager to explore that mysterious Eden with him,
Alys drew his dark head down to her breast in an
unconsciously moving gesture of yielding surrender to
the longing to give, for his pleasure and her own

'I want you so much, Alys,' he said on a deep groan
of desire, his lips moving against her breast, their
touch exciting her beyond bearing. 'I don't think I can
wait much longer. . .'

'I can't wait, either,' she breathed recklessly, on fire
with the longing he ignited, past caring for anything
but its fulfilment.

Needing no further assurance, Zack reared to his
feet and swept her up, his mouth clamping down hard
on welcoming lips. With her arms about his neck and
her heart thudding, Alys revelled in the ease with
which he carried her up to his bedroom and laid her in
the middle of a huge double bed.

He undressed her slowly, with many kisses and
loving caresses, taking pleasure in her pearly body
with its small but perfect breasts, narrow waist and
hips and long, shapely legs. The taut beauty of her
nudity delighted him beyond words and he buried his
warm lips in her breasts and moved slowly down the
length of her quivering body, sweeping passionate
kisses over every inch of her warm, sweet flesh to the
threshold of her throbbing womanhood.

Alys caught her breath at the shock of his lips in
that sensitive and very secret place and Zack smiled

with tender understanding and returned to kissing her breasts, lips and clever tongue teasing and tautening the nipples until she moaned with pleasure.

His mouth scorched her bare flesh with the feverish heat of his passion and she arched her body in sheer delight as he showered kisses upon her, fully aware of her increasing arousal and schooling the growing urgency of his own desire. She was so precious to him that he was taking great care to make this first time with him as magical and as memorable as he could.

Alys caressed the warm, muscular chest with its tendrils of curling dark hair and allowed her hand to wander in shy exploration over his body to the potent, thrusting shaft of his masculinity. She heard his sigh and felt him tense as she touched him, and as he said her name on an ache of desire she thrilled to her woman's power over this prince among men.

Her own resistance at nil, she craved the ultimate, sensuous lovemaking that was the inevitable outcome of the sizzling sexual awareness between them since her very first day in A and E. Liquid heat spiralling, she held him even closer and moved instinctively to facilitate his welcome invasion. . .

He was a skilful and sensitive lover, tender but necessarily urgent, sweeping her towards the desired culmination of their mutually feverish passion with each rhythmic thrust of powerful loins and the erotic gentling of her slender body with his clever hands.

Totally consumed by the moment, responding hungrily to the seeking warmth of his mouth and the rising urgency of his strong but controlled lovemaking, Alys gave herself totally to the new and delicious sensations and soon felt her whole being soar with astonished ecstasy to the towering peaks of physical delight and shudder to a mystical, magical crescendo in his embracing arms.

'I didn't know it would be like that!' she exclaimed ingenuously, on a mix of tears and laughter, hugging him out of sheer happiness as they lay beached on the shores of after-love.

'I knew from the moment I saw you that it would be exactly like that for us,' Zack murmured with a deep satisfaction — and then stiffened and raised himself on an elbow to look into her flushed and radiant face as he realised the import of the revealing words. 'It was your first time. . .' He ought to have realised but he had been too carried away with passion to heed a brief, involuntary resistance. Besides, she had been more responsive and more ready for him than many more experienced women, he thought on a surge of tenderness and love.

'Of course it was!' Alys returned with swift indignation that he could doubt it, but the spark of resentment died almost immediately. 'I thought you must have known. . .' She leaned to kiss him, smiling into his eyes with a little anxiety in her own. 'Does it matter?'

Alys wondered if she had disappointed him with a response that could only be instinctive, too inexperienced to know that their first lovemaking had surpassed his wildest dreams and confirmed his belief that she was the only woman he would want for the rest of his life.

'Darling, I feel privileged,' he said softly, enfolding

her in his arms once more, and her heart swelled with glad relief as the quiet words seemed to convey a much needed assurance that he cared for her far more than he was yet saying.

They made love again with a quiet, slow delight in each other that seemed even more magical than the urgency of that first encounter and, bathed in his protective and gentle loving, Alys fell even more deeply into love with him and knew she would love him to eternity and beyond, come what may.

Zack took her home just after midnight when she insisted that she couldn't spend the whole night in his arms, however tempted she might be.

'Someone would get to know and tell Martin,' she explained. 'And I think I owe him the right to hear from me that I've made a mistake.'

'Do you want me there?' he asked instantly, tenderly protective, knowing the CO's hot temper better than most.

Alys shook her head. 'That would only make matters worse. You must know how he feels about you!'

He smiled wryly. 'I think I get the general drift. . .'

She leaned towards him for a last kiss, breathlessly tender, heart filling and surging with love and a new optimism for the future. Surely no man could say so much with his kiss and the warm glow in his eyes if he didn't mean it!

She tiptoed past the bedrooms that contained her sleeping friends, her mouth swollen and tremulous from Zack's ardent kisses and her body still tingling with the unimagined delight of his lovemaking.

Stealing between the sheets, she hugged her pillow,

already missing Zack's arms about her, and wished he had spoken just one word to make her feel that she was loved. He had murmured compliments and endearments and sighed her name at the moment of supreme pleasure in her arms but she was still not sure that those memorable hours would lead to a long and lasting and mutually loving relationship.

She desperately needed to know that, as soon as she was freed from her foolish promise to Martin, the whole world would learn that she and Zack were lovers and Wanda would be compelled to accept that she was a part of his past. . .

Alys arrived for work the next morning to a buzz of excitement and the staggering shock of the news that the SCO and Sister Cas were definitely on the verge of matrimony. It appeared that one of Wanda's closest friends had confided in yet another friend that the casualty sister had finally come to an important decision about her future.

No one was saying that she was actually engaged to the SCO. But in her sensitive state of mind, Alys found it easy to believe that Wanda had made up her mind to marry Zack, and her heart sank all the way down to her sensible, flat-heeled shoes.

She was shaken and sick at heart but not surprised. In spite of his ardent lovemaking of the previous night and her experience of much exaggerated grapevine gossip, it seemed inevitable that he would marry the woman he claimed to have known all his life and had probably always loved.

What a fool she had been! Not only to fall into his arms like ripe fruit but to fall headlong into love with him, too! Well, a girl could fall out of love just as easily, Alys told herself with angry pride — and thankfully she hadn't confessed how she felt about him. Or yet told Martin that she couldn't marry him!

Now there was no need. An instinctive distrust of Zack had swept her into the security of that engagement and marriage must surely provide even more of a protection against loving the wrong man!

CHAPTER THIRTEEN

NICOLA looked round in surprise as Alys snapped at a junior. The good-natured staff nurse seemed to be in low spirits that morning. Time of the month, perhaps—and Alys *was* rushed off her feet in Wanda Nelson's continued absence.

At least Zack was back. It had been even more hectic when both he and Wanda were off duty. 'Alys coped very well,' she assured him when he asked how things had gone. 'She has all the makings of an excellent sister cas and I'll happily recommend her for the job if it becomes available.'

Like almost everyone else, she was itching to know if Wanda had agreed to marry him after months of wistful mourning for Martin and whether she meant to give up nursing for domesticity as a doctor's wife.

Zack arced a dark eyebrow. 'Is that likely? Is Wanda thinking of leaving?'

He knew she had been restless and unhappy at Benny's ever since her break with Kemp and it wouldn't surprise him if she had finally decided on a change. Particularly if she knew that the CO hoped to marry Alys. That engagement was destined to be one of the shortest on record but obviously Wanda couldn't know that.

'You're in a better position to know her plans than I am!' As her pager beeped to summon her to the nearest telephone, Nicola dashed away before he could question her sly smile.

Zack wondered what fresh rumours had been circulating in his brief absence and was enlightened a few minutes later when a radiologist congratulated him on his engagement.

'Nice of you but rather premature,' he said lightly. 'I haven't proposed to anyone yet.'

Ruth stared. 'But everyone says that you're engaged to Wanda!'

He smiled but he was appalled to think of Alys's reaction if she heard something so untrue and so unlikely. 'Well, I'm afraid everyone's got it wrong. I am hoping to get married in the near future but you've got the wrong woman.'

For weeks, he had allowed the rumours to run riot, but he had told Alys a number of times that Wanda was just an old friend. Now, realising how another and more serious story about himself and Wanda would hurt a modest girl who didn't yet know that she was loved, he cursed the decision to keep back the words she might have needed to hear.

He felt that his kisses and his content in her embrace should have convinced her that she was his one true love but he had meant to wait until she was free of that ridiculous commitment to Kemp before he asked her to marry him instead.

Now it was obviously vital to ease her possibly anxious mind and heart as soon as he could. A and E at its busiest time was scarcely the venue he could wish but it seemed he was left with no choice. . .

Alys ticked off each item on the drugs list as she

checked the phials and packets and hypodermic syringes newly delivered from Pharmacy. It was a task that needed care and concentration so she wasn't best pleased to be interrupted, not even by Zack.

He perched on the edge of the desk, swinging a long leg, tall and lean and handsome in the white coat with his stethoscope dangling from a deep pocket.

'How are you this morning, sweetheart?' he asked softly, a little concerned that she didn't look up with her swift, sweet smile.

Was she hurt and angry because she had heard the rumour that linked him afresh with Wanda's future? Or had she realised that she didn't care anything for him, after all, and was regretting something that might have lost her the man she still wanted to marry?

Zack simply didn't know the answers. . .

'Busy!' Alys returned briskly, head bent uncompromisingly over the register. She didn't need to look up at a man whose image was stamped indelibly on heart and mind.

'I suppose you've seen Martin this morning. How is he?' He tried to keep anxiety out of his tone but he desperately hoped that she had taken immediate steps to straighten things out.

'Improving.' Alys checked the label of a small plastic container, wishing his mere presence wouldn't quicken her heartbeat in such a foolish fashion. 'Doing so well that John Winter is talking of discharging him at the weekend although it will be some time before he'll be fit enough for work.'

'So all's well that ends well,' Zack suggested hopefully.

'So it seems,' she said stiffly, fancying she heard a note of satisfaction in his deep voice and thinking it must be true that he and Wanda were soon to be married. It hurt even to contemplate. 'Please don't tinker with those drugs, Zack!' Her tone was sharp. 'I haven't finished listing them!'

'Sorry. . .' He replaced the phial he had absently picked up to turn in restless fingers, needing to occupy hands that yearned to touch and hold her, desperately afraid that he had lost her with that impetuous love-making. She seemed so cool and distant, unlike the heart-warming lover of the previous night.

Alys felt the smart of tears and swallowed hard, too conscious of the nearness and the dearness of him and an ache in her breast for the death of a dream.

'Did you want something, Zack? Only I *am* trying to get this done. . .'

Zack wanted very much to kiss her but he doubted in her present prickly mood she would consider it an acceptable reason for interrupting her busy schedule. 'I need to talk to you, Alys,' he told her quietly.

Sure what he meant to admit, needing to put distance between them, she took a handful of packets and phials across the room and began to store them carefully in the drugs cabinet. 'I don't think I want to hear anything you have to say, Zack,' she said coldly, beginning to be angry. As a newly engaged man, he had no right to caress her with his velvet voice and tilt her heart with the warmth in his eyes!

Her retreat was expressive. Suddenly sure that she was reacting like any girl who had yielded her virginity without being sure she was loved, Zack crossed the room in two strides and turned her to face him with gentle hands.

'Then I won't bother with words. Perhaps this carries more conviction, anyway. . .' He cradled her head between his hands and kissed her, long and deep and fiercely impatient with her refusal to recognise his love and longing.

The world rocked as his warm mouth sent her senses spinning out of control. But Alys snatched at the remnants of her pride and thrust him away in a fury of outrage.

'Don't ever do that again or you'll find yourself on a charge of sexual harassment!' she stormed on a tempestuous impulse.

Zack paled at the threat that opened up a healing wound and then, as a junior nurse appeared at the open office door, he stalked from the room, filled with an unforgiving anger at the harsh words.

There had been such a blaze in his steel-grey eyes that Alys felt compelled to allay the first-year's obvious suspicion of the tense atmosphere and her flushed face.

'These arrogant doctors. . .!' she exclaimed brightly, forcing a smile, hoping the girl hadn't seen or heard any part of that exchange. 'Can't bear to have their theories challenged! I don't know one who'll accpet that a nurse might know more than they do!'

It was lame but the girl seemed to accept the explanation for Zack's angry departure, much to her relief. For the gossip-mongers were already having a field day and she had no wish to add to their delight.

She would have been very disturbed if she'd known

that the student nurse had seen and heard it all and went away to whisper to her friends what she had witnessed between the good-looking SCO and the senior staff nurse.

It was bad enough that Zack spoke to her only when forced to do so, obviously angered by that violent rejection and the ugly threat. Having meant to impress on him that she didn't welcome more of his lovemaking or his insincere flattery, it seemed that she had succeeded only too well and Alys was utterly miserable in the face of his cold, implacable distance.

If she had known about the unfounded accusation and subsequent enquiry that had driven him from Hartlake, she would have hastened to make amends. Instead, it seemed to her that he welcomed the rift in their relationship and she felt it was further proof, if she needed it, that he meant to marry Wanda and regretted a brief interlude in her arms.

It didn't help matters when Wanda returned to A and E looking like a cat who had been at the cream. Alys was so downcast that she was tempted to ask for a transfer to a ward or department where she wouldn't see Zack almost every day.

'Staff—Sister Cas wants you in the office—right away!' A first-year nurse stuck her head between the cubicle curtains to pass on the message.

'Very well, Nurse—thank you!' It sounded peremptory, even urgent, but Alys went on with the neat bandaging of a child's knee. A plaster over the two small sutures would probably have been sufficient but she sensed that the little boy wanted an obvious show of injury to impress his friends. 'There you are,

Jason—now you really look like a wounded soldier,' she assured him warmly.

'Can I go back to school?' he asked eagerly.

'I don't see why not. What does Mummy think?'

Jason's mother nodded, smiling. 'It wasn't as bad as his teacher thought,' she said thankfully, having been summoned by the school head to accompany her child to hospital.

'It bled a lot,' he said importantly.

'It *was* rather a deep cut.' Alys ran a hand over the child's short-cropped blond hair on a surge of tenderness. She was conscious of maternal feelings very often these days and she wondered if Zack had awakened more than her sexual awareness with his touch and his kiss. She had always liked children but never felt quite so strongly that she would like to have some of her own. Somehow, she couldn't visualise Martin as their father. . .

'I sent for you ten minutes ago!' Wanda snapped as Alys knocked lightly on the office door and walked into the room.

'I'm sorry, Sister.' No one knew if Wanda really was engaged to Zack or if it was just another false rumour and apparently no one had the courage to ask. But the casualty sister wasn't wearing a ring.

That didn't mean anything, Alys reminded herself. *She* had agreed to marry Martin but they had to wait until he left Benny's before they could set an official seal on the engagement that still bound her to him. He expected to be discharged by the weekend and she had agreed to spend a few days with him at his family home. She wasn't looking forward to it at all. She

knew she should feel that it was the beginning of a
lifetime of contentment with someone who cared for
her deeply but it was hard to ignore the fierce hunger
in her heart for another man. . .

'Close the door! I don't want the entire department
to hear,' Wanda said coldly.

Alys was surprised by the apparent need for
privacy, usual prelude to a scold. 'Is something wrong,
Sister?'

Wanda looked her over with hard eyes, having two
good reasons to delight in humbling a girl she had
never liked. Jealousy because she had sweet talked
Martin into an engagement at a time when he was too
ill to know what he was doing and anger that she had
hurt someone as kind and caring as Zack who was
unmistakably in love and suffering more than he would
ever admit.

'You ordered and received a consignment of drugs
from Pharmacy in my absence.' She went straight to the
point. 'Some of them are missing — amphetamines.'

Alys paled. She had been a nurse long enough to
understand the implication of the words. 'But that's
not possible!' she protested.

Wanda pushed the drugs register across the desk
towards her. 'These *are* your figures, aren't they? And
this is your signature?'

'Yes, of course it is — but — ' Alys broke off, horror
flooding her at a sudden, deeply disturbing thought.
Was it possible that *Zack*. . .?

She recalled that he had come into the office, sat on
the desk and toyed with the phials and packages while
she entered the new consignment of drugs into the

register. He *couldn't* have taken the amphetamines!
He just wasn't that kind of man. But he had been in
the room and they were the only two people who had
such easy access to the missing drugs.

'Well, Nurse Mackenzie?' Wanda's tone was sharp
with suspicion.

Alys stared down at the open register. 'They *were*
here. Look—I've entered two phials in the register!'
she exclaimed, clutching at straws.

Wanda's smile was coolly contemptuous. 'You
entered two phials, each containing sixty tablets, but
only one phial is in the cabinet and there's no record
of any being used. Not very clever of you, was it?'

'Are you suggesting that *I* took them?' Alys
demanded sharply, indignant.

'I'm merely asking you to account for them.' Wanda
hastily backtracked, having no intention of being
charged with false accusation. 'Sixty amphetamine
tablets are missing. Obviously I need an explanation.'

'Yes, of course! But they must be here. . .!'
Troubled, she flew to the drugs cabinet and began to
search the neatly stored contents with frantic fingers.

Wanda watched her with a sceptical gleam in her
dark eyes. 'I wish you joy of finding them. I certainly
couldn't!'

And nor could Alys for all her desperate searching.
She turned to look at the casualty sister with wide,
apprehensive eyes. 'What happens now?'

'I think you must know. The first step is to ensure
that you don't attend to any patients until it's decided
if you are to be suspended or can carry on with your
work.'

'Suspended!' Alys was horrified, for she cherished the hard-won badge she wore on her apron bib and couldn't believe that it was in jeopardy.

'The next step is to report the missing drugs to Matron and she'll obviously want to know if you can shed any light on the mystery. Go and take off your cap and apron and wait until she sends for you—and please don't leave the hospital precincts in the meantime.'

Feeling absurdly like a criminal, Alys left the room. The casualty sister's tone made it plain she didn't consider there was any mystery at all and she knew she was already tried and found guilty in Wanda's eyes.

But she hadn't taken the missing drugs and she didn't want to believe that Zack had purloined them so they had to be somewhere in the department. She had locked the drugs cabinet and kept the key on her until she went off duty so the phial of sixty amphetamines had obviously gone missing at some time when she wasn't responsible for its safe keeping.

Thankfully, her conscience was perfectly clear—and she would say so when she was summoned to Matron's office!

St Benet's had reverted to the more popular title of 'Matron' at the same time as it had gone back to caps and starched aprons after an experimental discard. It had been found that patients were reassured by the continuation of nursing traditions. But a rose by any other name had just as many thorns, as many a nurse discovered when summoned to answer for some sin to the crusty Miss Lorimer.

Nancy Lorimer had trained in the days when nurses combined medical care with ward-cleaning and a certain amount of food preparation and serving, and she had all the old-fashioned attitudes to the job. Benny's nurses lived by her rules or left to further their training at a different hospital.

Alys had made mistakes during her training just like every other junior nurse but she had been so obviously caring and conscientious that she had escaped the worst of Matron's censure. In fact, she had always felt a little favoured because Miss Lorimer had nursed with her mother and now she disliked the thought of appearing before her in disgrace.

'I expect you are well aware that this is a very serious charge, Nurse Mackenzie.'

'One of which I'm innocent, Matron!' It was hard not to sound heated when so much was at stake although Alys realised that vehemence was no proof of innocence. 'Oh, I've taken the occasional aspirin on a bad day—everyone does! But anything more than that—*never*!'

'Then what do you think has happened to the amphetamines, my dear?'

Alys shook her head, almost in despair although the kindly tone implied that Matron was inclined to believe her ardent denial. 'I wish I knew,' she said heavily.

Miss Lorimer tapped the register that lay open on the desk. 'You counted and entered each drug and signed the book as correct. Is that right?'

'Yes—and it *was*! I know it was.'

'But now a phial of sixty tablets cannot be found. What did you do with the key to the cabinet?'

'Kept it on the chain with the rest of the department keys until I was relieved, as usual.' She might have broken the occasional rule during her years at Benny's but that was one that every nurse knew better than to overlook.

'So you were the only person who had access to the missing tablets?'

Her heart sank. 'Yes. But that was yesterday morning. Anyone could have gone to the drugs cabinet in the meantime!'

'Can you think of anyone who might have helped themselves to amphetamines if they had the opportunity?'

A team of wild horses couldn't have dragged Zack's name from her although it instantly leaped to mind. Unfounded accusations were horrid—as she was finding to her cost!

She shook her head. 'None of the nurses,' she said firmly. 'I'm sure of that, Matron.' She couldn't imagine any nurse or CO misusing or stealing drugs, let alone Zack. But what was she to think?

'A patient, perhaps?' Miss Lorimer suggested.

'That's more likely, I suppose—but the cabinet is never left unlocked.'

'I know you were short-staffed yesterday and I expect the department was busy. Isn't it possible that the keys were left lying about in an absent-minded moment? Please be quite open with me, Nurse. It's in everyone's best interests to get to the bottom of this, isn't it?'

'Sister Nelson was off duty and one of the juniors went home with a migraine so we *were* short-staffed,'

Alys agreed. 'And A and E is always busy. But I had
the keys on me at all times.' Her eyes were troubled
as she met Miss Lorimer's gently questioning gaze. 'I
wish I could give you an explanation, Matron. I can
only repeat that the tablets were securely locked away
with the rest of the drugs and the keys never left my
keeping.'

'Very well. I'm sorry to say this, Nurse, but you do
realise that I cannot allow you back on duty until this
matter is resolved?' Nancy Lorimer was as distressed
as she sounded.

'I understand, Matron.'

With a sinking dread in the pit of her stomach, Alys
closed the door behind her and made her way back to
A and E to collect her things. Sister Wells's daughter
to be suspected of stealing drugs! It was an unthinkable
disgrace. . .

CHAPTER FOURTEEN

NICOLA intercepted her as she was about to leave the department. 'Going home, Alys?' Her tone was warmly sympathetic. 'You haven't looked well all day. Is there anything I can do? If you'd like to wait for just a few minutes while I finish with this patient, I'll take my break and run you home. . .'

Alys managed to smile in spite of the tears that were very close to the surface. 'I am going home but I must see Martin first,' she returned, allowing the CO to assume that she had been sent off duty because she wasn't well. She couldn't bear to admit the real reason to someone whose good opinion she valued. 'It's very nice of you, Nicola. But I won't encroach on your precious lunch-hour.'

'Sure. . .?' But she had already accepted the smiling refusal and hurried on, pausing only to confide her conviction that the staff nurse was deeply upset to the SCO.

Zack took one glance at the pale face of his dear love and immediately abandoned all thought of the patient he had been about to examine. Assigning that duty to the first available CO, he caught up with Alys just as she reached the outer doors.

'What's wrong?' he demanded, urgent with the desire to sweep her into his arms and kiss the shine of tears from her beautiful eyes.

She turned to look at him. 'I've been suspended,'
she said, doubting if it was any surprise to him. Even
if no one else did, Zack must know that she had been
summoned to Matron's office and why. For she felt
sure that Wanda had hurried to him with her tale of
missing drugs.

'Suspended! Why, for heaven's sake?' He scowled.

'Then Wanda hasn't told you?' Zack looked so blank
that she explained, as briefly as possible, for it was
humiliating to admit that she was under suspicion.

'What a load of rubbish!' he said angrily, leaping
instantly to her defence. 'You of all people! I can't
think why Wanda felt she had to bring Matron into it
at such an early stage when there must be a simple
explanation.'

Alys didn't dare to mention her staggering doubt
about his honesty. He would obviously deny that he'd
taken the amphetamines and would be unforgivingly
furious at being accused if he was as innocent as
herself; she shrank from being frozen by his implacable
anger again, however justified this time.

'She really didn't have a choice,' she said fairly.
'Missing drugs are about the worst crime in the book
and you know they have to be reported right away,
Zack.' Somehow, nothing seemed so bad now that he
was speaking to her again, showing his concern.

'But to accuse you. . .!' His handsome face was
stormy. 'I know what you must be feeling, having been
falsely accused myself in the past.'

'Of stealing drugs?' she exclaimed in astonishment.

He looked down at her with thoughtful eyes. 'I
thought Kemp went out of his way to tell you that I

faced a charge of sexual harassment shortly before
leaving Hartlake.'

Alys went cold with shock. Recalling the taunt she'd
thrown at him in an absurd gesture of self-defence, it
was painfully evident why he'd been so angry and she
was appalled that he should think her so cruel and
insenistive.

'No! If he knew, he didn't tell me! You surely don't
think I'd have said such an awful thing to you the other
day if I'd known. . .!'

'Your remark rather took my breath away at the
time, I must admit.' His eyes warmed as the last trace
of angry disappointment melted before her very transparent horror. 'It seemed so unlike you.'

'You were innocent, of course,' she said stoutly,
without an atom of doubt in her own mind.

Zack was touched by her trust. Briefly, in as few
words as possible for his time was limited, he told her
something of those difficult weeks of his own suspension and the subsequent enquiry that had cleared his
name completely.

'What a wicked woman!' Alys exclaimed hotly.

'She was a very lonely and unhappy woman,' he
amended quietly, and she loved him all the more for
his insight and compassion. He glanced at his watch. 'I
don't want you to worry about a thing, Alys,' he swept
on, suddenly determined. 'I'll sort this business out for
you!'

He swung on his heel to head for the office and Alys
would have been less than human not to feel her spirits
lift at his championing of her cause.

Zack *would* sort things out if he could, she knew.

He was that kind of man, caring, concerned and considerate. Patients trusted him and colleagues relied on him — and even the least susceptible of nurses found it hard to resist the lure of his quiet charm. Alys had found it impossible for her heart not to thaw before a warm and tender pursuit that had convinced her that she was really special in his eyes.

Realising that he had said not one word to dispel her belief that he was planning to marry Wanda, she was saddened that it had possibly all been a lie. . .

Before going home, she made her way to the NSU, but she had no intention of telling Martin about the missing drugs or her suspension from duty. She only had one thing on her mind as she pushed open the swing doors of the unit and that was to explain that she couldn't marry him.

Alys had never wanted to hurt him and she would probably miss his loving support in the difficult weeks ahead if she couldn't prove to everyone's satisfaction that she knew nothing about the missing amphetamines. She might need him even more when Zack married Wanda Nelson. But he deserved better than a wife who loved another man with all her heart. . .

John Winter had just finished examining his patient when she peeped into the side-ward. He turned to greet her with a warmly welcoming smile. 'There you are, Nurse Mackenzie! I've some good news for you this morning. I'm so pleased with your young man's rapid recovery that I'm allowing him to go home even earlier than promised. Tomorrow, in fact.'

'I've just been telling John that I've the best reason in the world to get out of here,' Martin said, capturing her hand, visibly making an effort. 'It means regular check-ups for some time but at least I can stop playing the patient and get back to being a doctor again. And we can get around to buying you a ring for this finger. . .'

'There's plenty of time to think about that,' Alys demurred, rather too quickly. A flicker of surprise and suspicion crossed his blue eyes and she hurried on, 'It's wonderful that you've got on so well!' She turned to the neurosurgeon with a slightly strained smile. 'You've worked wonders!'

'Very little of it is due to me,' John Winter returned, admiring her prettily flushed face with the eye of a connoisseur. 'Rest and peace of mind has done the trick — and your regular visits, of course. I wish I could prescribe your particular brand of medicine for all my patients.'

She sat down beside the bed as the specialist went away to continue his round, nerving herself to face Martin's inevitable dismay and disappointment. 'Do you really feel well enough to go home so soon, Martin?' she asked anxiously, for he seemed a long way from his usual ebullient self.

'I'm fine,' he assured her stoutly. 'And I'm looking forward to taking you to meet my family and making plans for the future.' He squeezed her hand and added brightly, 'What better way to convalesce?'

Alys looked down at the hands he clutched with the lingering of a dependence he had shown ever since the accident and wondered if she could find the courage — or the lack of heart — to confess that she didn't want

to meet his family or make plans for a future he
confidently expected them to share.

And was there really any need now that all her
foolish dreams of spending her life with Zack had been
shattered so painfully? She might find a safe harbour
for her troubled heart with Martin and perhaps she
could learn to love him in time. . .

The momentary hesitation was banished by the
fierce protest of her heart, for she could never gladden
at Martin's touch or thrill to his kiss or know the rare
magic that had surrounded her as she lay in Zack's
tender embrace. Loving him had been her inescapable
destiny and that brief idyll in his arms was a rare gold
thread in the tapestry of her life, a bright ray of
sunshine made all the more precious because of the
shadow of another woman's apparent claim to him.

She withdrew her hands on the pretext of picking up
a book that had slipped from the bed to the floor. 'I
don't think we should be in too much of a hurry to
make plans, Martin,' she said gently, paving the way
as carefully as she could to spare his feelings, for she
knew that any setback in cases of serious head injury
could have disastrous results. 'There'll be time enough
to discuss dates and look at rings when you're really fit
again.'

Martin searched her guarded face with narrowed
eyes and something akin to relief in his breast. 'You've
changed your mind,' he said quietly.

Alys didn't even attempt a denial. 'Things happened
in such a rush. I never meant to get so involved or to
make promises I knew I couldn't keep.' Her hazel eyes
were filled with contrition. 'I'm so sorry, Martin. . .'

He didn't seem surprised or particularly dismayed. 'I knew it wasn't what you wanted,' he admitted generously. 'I pushed you into saying you'd marry me because I didn't want to give Zack the satisfaction of stepping into my shoes as he did with Wanda. But I've been fighting a losing battle all these weeks, haven't I? You're in love with him.'

It was statement rather than question and Alys nodded rueful agreement, thankful that he had taken it so well. 'I really am sorry,' she murmured.

He patted her hand. 'Don't look so troubled, Alys. You haven't broken my heart. Bruised it a bit, perhaps. But I've had plenty of time to think, lying here, and I've had some doubts of my own. As you say, things happened too fast. . .'

He was too forgiving, too understanding, heaping coals of fire on her humbled head. 'Oh, Martin. Now I really do feel dreadful,' she wailed.

'No need. I've never really thought of myself as the marrying kind, to be honest. That's where things went wrong with Wanda. . .'

Hearing the rueful note in his tone, Alys wondered if he regretted that break with Wanda more than *her* lack of love for him. 'I expect you know that she's engaged to Zack,' she said tentatively.

He laughed. 'That old chestnut!'

'It seems to be true this time.'

'Wanda's told me all about her plans for the future and they certainly don't include marrying Zachary Howes,' Martin said confidently.

'Then she's been to see you?' Alys was surprised — and heartened, for surely he would know if Wanda was telling the truth. Her heart soared on another wild flight of fancy and hope.

'Of course.' Martin released her hand and lay back against the pillows. 'We were very close at one time,' he reminded her. 'I think she's still very fond of me. . .'

He sounded so gratified that it was easy to believe that he cared for Wanda in spite of the events of recent weeks. Deeply thankful to be freed from an engagement she had never wanted, Alys soon took her leave of him, convinced that the speed of his recovery owed more to the casualty sister's visits than her own half-hearted concern. If only she could believe that they might get together again if she and Zack faded from the scene!

Arriving home, instead of a flatmate sleeping peacefully in her own room she found a note from Sally pinned to the kitchen board. Some friends had invited her to spend her off-duty nights with them in the nearby coastal town and she had decided to accept. She had written:

Lots of sun and sea and sand are just what I need. Sorry about the laundry but I just didn't have time once Paul and Linda phoned. What do you think about Sister Cas going to work in a clinic in New York — or is it still Benny's best-kept secret in spite of the grapevine? So much for that stupid story about her marrying Zachary Howes at last! I thought you'd be pleased to hear that there's absolutely no truth in it, Alys. . .

Alys read the note three times before the words sank in and then she still didn't know whether to believe her friend's well-meant assurances.

Was it possible that Wanda had led everyone up the garden path — including Zack? And why *America*? Did she want to put as many miles as possible between herself and Benny's? And, most important of all, how did Zack feel about the plans she had apparently confided to Martin — and were they really just the good friends of many years' standing that he had always insisted?

It was all theory and speculation, she warned the heart that was beginning to weave impossible dreams, changing her uniform for a bright yellow tracksuit. As she put the familiar light blue, white collared dress of a Benny's staff nurse away in the wardrobe, she wondered when and if ever she would wear it again.

She devoted some of her unexpected free time to essential laundry and housework. She had always shared the chores with Wynne and Sally but it seemed painfully obvious that she would have plenty of time to do more than her share in the coming days unless Zack could mend matters on her behalf.

In the early afternoon, she answered an impatient ring of the doorbell and was startled to see the SCO standing on the step.

'Why didn't you let me know that you intended to come home?' he demanded without ceremony. 'I thought you'd wait until I'd had a word with Wanda, at least!'

Alys stepped back before the onslaught of the words, feeling threatened by the sheer height and power of his tall, broad-shouldered frame until she realised that the only threat was to her resistance, never at its best when he was around. Both heart and body had succumbed to the conviction that he was a man to love and to trust with her lasting happiness.

She led the way to the kitchen where she had been preparing a casserole to pop into the oven for the evening meal. 'There didn't seem to be any point in staying when I just didn't see how you could help. But I didn't leave right away. I went to the NSU to talk to Martin.' She hoped he would promptly take her up on the hint of the words.

Zack knew he should have realised that she would rush to the man she loved at a time of trouble but his heart sank. 'Doing well, isn't he? I gather he'll be out of hospital by the weekend.'

'Tomorrow,' she amended. 'John Winter told him this morning.'

'You must be very pleased.'

He seemed as distant as a stranger, this man whose lean, hard body she had known so intimately, exulting in the race of his heart and the tumult and the thrust of his loins, soaring with him to paradise.

'Naturally. . .and relieved that there weren't any complications. . .' For Zack's sake, as he must surely realise.

'So it's full steam ahead with the wedding plans, is it?' His heart wrenched at the thought of her as Kemp's bride, radiant vision in gown and veil.

'No.'

Zach looked at her quickly. 'Planning a long engagement, are you?'

'There isn't an engagement. Not any more.'

He couldn't be sure if it was regret or relief in her quiet voice. 'I hope that isn't my fault,' he said gently.

Alys frowned. 'Your fault?'

'The other night.'

'Oh. . .' She blushed with pleasure in the cherished memory of his arms about her and the rapture of his lovemaking. 'No. There was no need for Martin to know anything about that. I just told him that I knew I'd made a mistake.'

'You really don't want to marry him?' he asked quietly.

'I never did. Not really.'

There was no doubting the simple truth of the words. 'You seem to have a knack for getting yourself into scrapes, Nurse Mackenzie,' Zack mocked gently, teasing the impetuous nature that was so much a part of the warm-hearted and generous girl he loved.

'Coffee. . .?' Alys reached for the kettle, needing to be doing something to dispel the sudden tension between them as his smile lifted her heart and quickened her pulses with its reassuring thankfulness that her foolish engagement was at an end. Her mouth was dry with nervous excitement and she was sure he must hear the unsteady, betraying thud of her heart.

Zack leaned against the door-frame, hands plunged in his pockets, watching as she plugged in the kettle and took a coffee jar from a cupboard. Having delayed just long enough to arrange for a colleague to cover for him, he had left a department full of waiting patients to be with her. He couldn't wait to hold her in his arms — and she offered him coffee!

He moved out of her way as she stretched to take mugs from a wooden stand and his glance fell on the wall-board with its jumble of notes and cards and shopping lists. Sally's words leaped at him with their reference to his own name — and, slightly above it, Wanda's. He leaned forward to read them and his eyes narrowed in surprise.

'So that's what she was up to!' he exclaimed.

Alys turned to look at him. 'What. . .?'

'Wanda.' He indicated the note. 'She spent most of the week in London. She must have gone for an interview for this job.'

'Then it's true that she's going to America?' So they *hadn't* been together during those days when everyone said they were making wedding arrangements. And if that rumour had no foundation in fact, perhaps all the others about him and Wanda were false, too — and she had been sick at heart for nothing!

'I've no idea. But I suppose it's possible. She's been rather secretive lately and kept hinting that she might not be around much longer. I thought she meant that there was someone new in her life.'

'So you went out looking for someone new?' Alys suggested, doing her best to tease but only managing to sound accusing although weeks of getting close to him had done much to dispel her distrust.

Grey eyes suddenly turned to steel. 'Is that really what you think? That I needed someone to replace Wanda in my life and thought you'd do very nicely? Kemp's poison seems to be insidious stuff.'

'Don't blame Martin,' she said quickly. 'If only half

the rumours about you are true, you earned your reputation!'

'Years ago,' he said grimly, wondering if he would ever win the heart of a girl who seemed so determined to think the worst of him. 'And it seems likely to cost me dear!'

CHAPTER FIFTEEN

ZACK stalked from the room before she could question the bitter tone. Quietly considering his words and ready with all her heart to believe that he was much misjudged, Alys made the coffee and carried the tray into the living-room. Zack stood by the window, hands thrust deep into trouser pockets, stiff as a ramrod with hurt and anger, and she wished she could simply walk over to him and put her arms about him with love.

'I'm sorry. I didn't mean to offend you,' she said penitently. 'I seem to be always saying and doing the wrong thing where you're concerned.'

He felt his heart contract as he saw the flush of colour in her pretty face and the wariness in her lovely eyes and suddenly knew that she was afraid of being hurt rather than afraid of being involved.

'Perhaps we can start saying the right things to each other from now on,' he suggested on a rush of protective tenderness for his vulnerable love, anger dissolved by the sweetness of her smile. 'Anyway, I said I'd sort out this amphetamine business for you — and I have.'

'You *have* — but how?'

Delight mingled with disbelief in her heart-shaped face and it took all Zack's strength of mind to keep from reaching out for her. She was so pretty, so slim and youthful in her brightly coloured tracksuit, her hazel eyes widening and brightening and her mouth shaping an O of surprise.

'I've talked to Matron and seen the drugs register and checked the entries with the pharmacy list, as Wanda should have done before leaping to absurd conclusions. Silly girl, you entered that phial of tablets *twice*. That's why one appeared to be missing,' he said gently, waiting for the dawn of comprehension and the flood of relief to her beautiful eyes with a tenderly teasing smile in his own.

Alys instantly realised the mistake, such an obvious one if only she'd had time to think. While he was sitting on the edge of the desk, his restless hands had picked up a phial of tablets she had already listed and put to one side and then restored it to the wrong pile when she snapped at him. In her flurry of confusion and upset, she had entered it twice in the register without realising.

She couldn't blame Wanda for suspecting her so wrongly and failing to check with Pharmacy. She couldn't really blame Zack for distracting her in the middle of such an important task. She was entirely to blame for being so much in love with the charismatic SCO that he could muddle her usually level head and interfere with the work so dear to her heart and turn her whole world upside-down.

'Are you sure. . .?' She scarcely dared to believe that the threatened nightmare of disgrace and dismissal wasn't about to happen.

'Wanda and I have been through the whole procedure and checked with Pharmacy to confirm exactly what was delivered. It was a stupid mistake but no more than that — and I expect it was my fault in more ways than one,' he added ruefully. 'I gather that Matron means to contact you to ask you to return to work in the morning.'

'I don't know what to say. . .' She sent him a wavery smile of relief. Until that moment, she hadn't known quite how much it meant to be cleared of such a career-threatening suspicion. Nursing was her whole life — or at least it had been until she met and fell deeply in love with this confidently smiling doctor!

'You don't have to say anything.' He fought the storm of longing to sweep her into arms that ached to hold her. 'I think I've said it all for you — and it will probably be some time before Wanda forgives me for some of it but I was absolutely furious that she gave you no chance at all to work out what had happened between you. If she and I could clear up the mystery so easily then obviously you could have done so, too.'

'You don't seem too concerned about upsetting Wanda,' Alys ventured lightly.

'I was much more concerned that she'd upset you. Remembering what it was like for me to be suspected of something I hadn't done and wouldn't dream of doing — well, I couldn't let you go through that a moment longer than necessary.'

He sounded so concerned, so caring and protective of her, that Alys suddenly knew that it wouldn't matter in the least if Wanda stayed at Benny's or went to Timbuktu!

'I was so afraid I'd lose my job,' she admitted. Leaving Benny's under a cloud would probably have meant never seeing Zack again — and how could she have borne that when her whole being yearned and throbbed with love for him and her heart was suddenly singing with the hope that the warm glow in his smiling eyes promised all that a woman could possibly want? 'I just don't know how to thank you, Zack. . .'

'You can thank me later,' he told her with a gleam of mischief in his grey eyes that brought the hint of a blush to her cheeks. He lowered his tall frame into an armchair and crossed one long leg over the other, reaching for the coffee she had made for him. 'But first there are a few misunderstandings that we need to sort out, Alys. For one thing, now you know that Wanda means to leave Benny's, perhaps you'll believe that we are not lovers and never have been.'

His firm tone held the ring of truth and Alys was more than ready to believe him and to regret that she had ever doubted his integrity. 'Then she wasn't punishing me because she knew that you liked me?'

It was so much more than liking, he thought tenderly, but it wasn't yet the moment to say so. 'No. It was your relationship with Kemp that she found so hard to take. Losing him almost broke her heart.'

'I didn't realise that she cared about him that much.'

'I doubt if anyone did. She isn't the kind to wear her heart on her sleeve. She's proud and stubborn but she isn't really spiteful by nature, so now you know why she's been treating you so badly perhaps you can forgive her?'

'You must be very fond of her to plead her cause so fervently.' It wasn't easy to keep the still-flickering flame of jealousy from her eyes and voice for she still wasn't totally sure of his feelings.

'We grew up as close as brother and sister and I've never had the slightest desire to marry her, whatever the gossips might say,' he said firmly. 'She helped me through some bad times — when Jenny died and later with that business at Hartlake — and I hope I've been able to help her through the heartache of losing Kemp in return. There was never anything more to our relationship than that.'

'If she has lost him.' Alys drank some of her own coffee and looked at Zack through the veil of her long, thick lashes. 'I think he may be missing her. He certainly wasn't broken-hearted when I said I didn't want to marry him.'

Zack shook his head. 'I think it's too late to salvage anything of that affair. Wanda took it very badly that he was so anti-marriage where she was concerned but asked you to marry him, and I doubt if she can forgive him for that. I don't know if she still loves him but if she's really serious about this job in America, then perhaps she means to make a completely fresh start.' He smiled at her tenderly. 'Perhaps we can too, Alys. All I ask is that you trust me.'

'I do. . .' Covered with confusion as she met the warm pleading in his remarkable eyes, Alys got up to take his empty cup from him. As their hands touched in the exchange, she felt the familiar tingle of a longing that owed far more to a real and lasting love than the physical response to his looks and charm and exciting maleness. 'I don't know why I said such a silly thing when I *like* being sexually harassed by you,' she added with a soft little laugh, and was rewarded by the swift amusement that leaped to lighten his grave expression.

'I was too angry even to talk to you — and then, thinking about the sweet girl I'd loved almost since the first day I met her, it just wasn't possible to believe that you wanted to hurt me and I knew you couldn't have known what you were saying.'

The loving words and his smiling eyes told Alys that she was just as special to him as he'd implied with that tender and memorable lovemaking and she was flooded with relief and a new-found joy.

Suddenly sure that she could reveal her heart without fear of rebuff or rejection, she bent down to kiss him, sliding her arms about his neck and smiling her heartfelt thankfulness before she kissed him again.

Zack got to his feet, towering above her, and looked down at her radiantly pretty face with a dancing but infinitely tender amusement in his grey eyes. 'Is this gratitude?' he drawled, with the slow, gently mocking but never malicious smile that had stolen her heart long before she knew it.

Alys leaned against him with her head on his broad chest and felt that the arms that promptly embraced her were a lifelong sanctuary. Her heart had come out of the cold and into the safe keeping of a man she was sure she could trust with her happiness for the rest of her life.

'No,' she said softly. 'I'm afraid it's love.'

His arms tightened about her and he dropped a kiss on the thick blonde curls that framed the lovely, heart-shaped face he had found himself dreaming about at the most unlikely moments even before he knew that he had fallen deeply in love for the first and definitely the last time in his life.

'You do realise that I shall want you to marry me?' His gaze held a great deal of tender love as he smiled down at her. 'I'm tired of providing the juniors with something to talk about and they'll lose interest once they find out that my intentions towards you are strictly honourable.'

Alys sighed her happiness against his heart but she still needed to be totally sure of what his eyes and his smile were saying. 'Are they? You aren't just stringing me along, Zack?'

'You still don't trust me, do you?' He shook his handsome head in mock-reproach. 'What will it take to convince you that I love you more than anything in the whole wide world?'

There was enough conviction for even the most doubting heart in the tender tone that turned the light words into a vow. But Alys still hesitated. 'Perhaps if you kissed me. . .?' she suggested with a little imp of provocation in her beautiful hazel eyes.

And happily lifted her face for the loving touch of his warm lips that would set the seal on a promise of a happiness that was sure to last their lifetime and beyond.

For he had shown her the path to paradise with his love and his warm and caring concern. . .

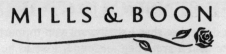